GLASBY, John
Death comes calling

This book must be returned by the last date stamped above.
Rhaid dychwelyd y llyfr hwn erbyn y dyddiad diwethaf a stampiwyd uchod.

A charge will be made for any lost, damaged or overdue books.
Codir tâl os byd... ...eb ei ddychwelyd
mewn pryd.

DEATH COMES CALLING

In Los Angeles, the wealthy Marcia Edwards asks investigator Johnny Merak to find her missing grandson. Merak suspects it's a mob kidnapping. There's someone else who wants to hire him: the model Angela Cliveden, who has been receiving life-threatening phone calls. Merak discovers that she is the girlfriend of Tony Minello of the local Mafia. But when she is found murdered in her apartment, Merak is trapped in a potential Mob War and matching his wits with a cunning serial killer.

JOHN GLASBY

DEATH
COMES
CALLING

Complete and Unabridged

LINFORD
Leicester

First published in Great Britain

First Linford Edition
published 2009

British Library CIP Data

Glasby, John
    Death comes calling.—Large print ed.—
Linford mystery library
    1. Gangsters—Fiction 2. Murder—Investigation—
Fiction 3. Detective and mystery stories
    4. Large type books
    I. Title
    823.9'12 [F]

ISBN 978–1–84782–568–1

Published by
F. A. Thorpe (Publishing)
Anstey, Leicestershire

Set by Words & Graphics Ltd.
Anstey, Leicestershire
Printed and bound in Great Britain by
T. J. International Ltd., Padstow, Cornwall

This book is printed on acid-free paper

1

It was a little after eight in the evening and I was sitting on my usual stool at the bar in Mancini's hoping I might bump into Sergeant Kolowinski. Business had been busy for a time but for the past few days there had been nothing apart from a couple of guys looking for errant wives who had strayed from the marital home and some dame who believed her husband was planning to murder her.

Since I soon discovered he'd run off with a rich widow and was now living in luxury in Hawaii I was able to assure her she was in no danger of being murdered. She wasn't too pleased about the Hawaii bit but I guess it was better than being smothered in your sleep or having strychnine put into your morning coffee.

I figured it was possible that Kolowinski might be able to throw something in my direction. We'd known each other for several years and in the past he'd proved

1

helpful in providing me with a little useful information — something the cops were stuck with and hadn't any real leads to go on.

The bartender sidled over, lifted my glass, and wiped the counter with a cloth before putting the bourbon down again. There was no sign of Kolowinski but as I glanced over the barkeep's shoulder I saw the door at my back reflected in the mirror behind the bar. It opened and someone came in. Whoever it was, it was certainly not Jack Kolowinski. She stood for a moment looking around her. Then she stepped inside, letting the door swing shut behind her.

One look was enough to tell me she wasn't the usual kind of broad who frequented places like Mancini's. Medium height, aged around sixty, she had silvery hair neatly waved. She had a pleasant face and could have been anybody's mother. I could picture her seated in a rocker on the stoop of some place way out in the country with a cluster of grandchildren around her feet.

Her outfit was elegantly styled and I

reckoned it hadn't come from any department store. She was someone important but I couldn't remember having seen her face in any of the newspapers or glossy magazines.

She looked around her in a kind of timid way as if she'd just figured she must be in the wrong place and was wondering how to get out of it without being noticed. I kept watching her and after a few moments she seemed to make up her mind. Something was bothering her and now she had to go through with whatever had led her into the bar.

My first thought was that she was looking for some prodigal son who had taken the wrong road, hoping to find him propping up some counter in a downtown bar. But as so often happened, events were soon to prove me wrong. She walked over and seated herself delicately on the stool next to me.

In a low voice, she asked, 'Excuse me, but are you Mister Merak — the private detective?'

She wasn't too different to some of the clients I'd had in the past — dames looking for straying husbands or wanting a divorce from someone they'd got tired of. But such dames normally came to my office, not to a bar like Mancini's.

'That's my name,' I told her. 'You have something on your mind? It must be something urgent to come here.'

'I realize that but I have to talk to you. I should have waited until tomorrow but I'm sure I'm being followed and if I went to your office, they'd know.'

She fumbled for a moment in the expensive handbag and then leaned forward to catch the bartender's eye.

I knew he'd been watching her closely ever since she'd walked in but at the moment he was busy talking to one of the other customers. He jumped when I rapped loudly on the bar and hurried over. 'What would you like to drink?' I asked her.

'Well, I — ' she hesitated.

'A brandy,' I said. 'Straight. And another bourbon on the rocks for me.'

When it came she sipped it slowly. Putting it down, she said, 'I know this isn't the usual place to discuss things but — '

I noticed the ring on her finger. 'Go ahead, Mrs. — ?'

'Edwards, Marcia Edwards.'

I nodded. 'As I was going to say, in my business even a bar like this is sometimes my office.'

I turned slowly to face her. Those little mice had woken up at the mention of her name and were now running around inside my mind. Marcia Edwards, reputedly the richest woman in the whole of L.A. Seldom seen outside the large mansion on the hill — almost as reclusive as Enrico Manzelli, the big boss who ran all of the underworld organizations. There, of course, the similarity ended. From all I knew, she was perfectly legit and had no connection with any of the gangs.

'You can speak freely here, Mrs. Edwards,' I told her. 'All of these people have their own worries and aren't interested in yours. But maybe we should go over to the table.'

I led her to the table furthest away from

the bar and the pool table at the end. Once she was seated, she said softly. 'I desperately need your help, Mister Merak. It's my grandson. He's been kidnapped.'

'May I ask how old he is?'

'He's only twelve. He's never been away from home before. God alone knows what he's suffering right now.' She took out a white silk handkerchief and wiped her eyes.

'I see. Just take your time, Mrs. Edwards. Have you received a ransom note? Have any of the kidnappers contacted you at all?'

She shook her head. 'It isn't like that. This isn't the usual case of kidnapping. You see I know who's taken him.'

I let that sink in, finally saying, 'I'm afraid I don't understand. If you know who's taken him, surely this is a matter for the cops.'

'I can't go to them. It's my son-in-law who's taken him, William's father.' I sat back. Things were beginning to get more confusing by the minute. I knew it wasn't the drink that was making it difficult for me to see things clearly. At the moment, there was something here that didn't make sense.

Finally, when she remained silent, I said, 'Surely if the boy's father has taken him, he'll be quite safe. Besides, the father is perfectly entitled to have his son with him unless your daughter goes to court for total custody.'

'That isn't the problem. My son-in-law is Charles Kenton. No doubt you've heard of him.'

I whistled through my teeth. Kenton was also a very big man in L.A. politics, very close to the Governor. He would certainly have a big pull with many important people.

'I must say I wasn't happy when my daughter married him.' Mrs. Edwards said after a pause. 'I suppose I had my suspicions then as to the kind of man he is. Now I've had those suspicions confirmed.'

'In what way?' I signalled to the bartender for another couple of drinks.

'I'd never really liked him from when he first moved into our family home. A few months ago I hired a private detective to investigate Charles Kenton. On the surface he's whiter than white. He's an ambitious man and intends to run for governor so it's important he should protect his image.

'The man I hired discovered that Kenton is deeply involved with several of the gang bosses. He arranges lucrative deals for them and I suppose they do the same for him in return. He's also a heavy gambler and already he's quite a few million dollars in debt to them and some are getting impatient to collect what he owes them. I confronted him about what I'd found out, and insisted that he leave my house. I made him give up his keys to me, and he is now living in his own apartment.'

'I take it you're suggesting he married your daughter purely for money and whatever political influence the Edwards name might bring.'

'Exactly.'

'And does your daughter know any of this?'

'I think for some time she's suspected

that something was wrong but he's very clever at concealing things. I haven't told her yet what this detective discovered. She's so much in love with him I'm sure she wouldn't believe me. Notwithstanding, I have seen to it that she has reverted to her maiden name, and severed all ties with Kenton. I've instructed my lawyers to see what can be done to expedite divorce proceedings, but in the meantime the courts have given Ginella custody of her son.'

'I understand, Mrs. Edwards. But you realize that if I take your case, I'll have to talk to her sooner or later?'

'I appreciate that, but I'd prefer it was later rather than sooner.'

I took a sip of my drink, studying her over the rim of the glass. Putting it down, I said, 'So what you're telling me is that your son-in-law has got your grandson hidden away somewhere and now he's using him as a weapon against you and your daughter.'

'That's partly correct. My belief is that he's arranged with these people to take William and conceal him somewhere.

He'll deny that, of course. And he'll have made certain there's no proof of anything linking him with them. But if he thinks he's going to get any money out of us, he's mistaken. I'll expose him first — let the public see just what kind of a crook he really is.'

Her bright blue eyes glinted behind the glasses she wore and quite suddenly she went from a typical all-American old lady to a hard, ruthlessly determined woman.

'That could be dangerous — for both of you. If he's as desperate for money as you believe, and these hoodlums are determined to get their money back, it could also put your grandson in even further danger.' I swallowed half of my drink. It was certainly an intriguing case but there were still a number of dangling loose ends that didn't tie up.

'You say you've already hired a private detective, so why come to me?'

She had her answer ready. 'Because the minute this private eye discovered the Underworld was in cahoots with Kenton, he backed out. He didn't want anything more to do with it. Afraid for his own skin if he went poking around too deeply.'

'And what makes you think I'd be any better?'

She smiled a little at that. 'I know you were once in one of these organizations yourself before you decided to go straight. I know you carry a gun in that shoulder holster and you're not afraid to use it whenever you have to.'

'You seem to know quite a lot about me.'

'I make it my business to know everything about anyone I ask for help. I'm a very wealthy woman and whatever your normal fees are, I'll double them if you try to find my grandson. Once I get him back safely, I know how to deal with Kenton and his cronies.'

I believed her. I could picture her sitting in the front of a prairie schooner, heading into the west, ready to take on Indians, outlaws and any other dangers that might lie ahead. 'All right,' I said. 'I'll do my best to find your grandson. Do you have a recent photograph of him?'

She opened her handbag and took out a photograph. I reckoned the boy was about nine or ten years old. So it would have been taken not too long before. He had curly blond hair and was grinning broadly at whoever had taken the picture. A kid without a care in the world, I thought.

'Thank you, Mister Merak.' She finished her drink and set the glass down on the table. Rummaging again inside her handbag she took out an envelope and laid it on the table beside my drink. 'There's ten thousand dollars in there, together with my address and telephone number.'

Without a further word, she got up and left.

I picked up the envelope and stuffed it into my pocket.

Mancini drifted over and stood looking down at me. 'That another of your clients, Johnny?' He grinned. 'And don't tell me it was your long-lost mother. Nobody who comes in here ever had a mother like that.'

I grinned. 'Another thing's certain. You never had.'

I finished my drink and went outside. It

was bitterly cold, the stars were brilliant, and the streets were filled with the night people, those who frequented all-night bars, girlie shows and gambling joints but were seldom seen during the day.

I thought about going back to my place — or Dawn's. But I needed time in which to clear my head. There was something about Mrs. Edwards that puzzled me and I couldn't figure out what it was. I knew very little about her son-in-law, Charles Kenton apart from his political ambitions.

Yet would even a man as ruthless as that allow his son to be murdered? I knew that if he didn't do exactly as he was told, there were men who wouldn't hesitate in killing the kid. I'd met men who would skin their own grandmother if it suited them but somehow I couldn't see Kenton being one of them.

I finished up at my own place, made myself a hot black coffee with a slug of whiskey in it and drank it before sliding between the sheets. Tomorrow was another day and by then I might have sorted things out a little better in my mind. Dawn was already in the office as I went in and tossed my hat onto the peg near the door. She glanced obliquely at me as I sank into the chair and swung my legs up onto the desk.

'A bad night, Johnny?' she asked.

'You could say that. I met up with this little old lady who wants me to find her grandson.'

'Sounds like a straightforward case.' She poured out a couple of cups of coffee and brought them over to the desk. Seating herself on the edge of the desk, she swung her legs around. 'So what's bothering you?'

'It appears that her grandson has been kidnapped by his father who has several of the mobs breathing down his neck, threatening to kill the boy unless he pays up. The trouble is that neither the wife nor her mother intend to help him.'

'Not even to save the boy's life?'

I shook my head. 'Seems this little old lady is banking on me finding him before they carry out their threat.'

Dawn was silent for several minutes, sipping her coffee. There was the usual worried expression on her face that appeared whenever I mentioned the mobs.

'Adding to the complications, the boy's father happens to be Charles Kenton,' I continued.

'The guy who hopes to run for governor?'

'The very same. Mrs. Edwards is a very determined old lady. She's threatening to expose Kenton the minute I find her grandson — and that isn't going to be easy.'

'Does she realize the danger she and her daughter could be in the moment she does that?'

I nodded. 'She does. But she comes from old Virginian stock and I'm afraid she'll do it and to hell with the consequences.'

I made to say something more but at that moment I picked out the sound of high heels coming along the corridor. A moment later, there came a knock on the door. It was a hesitant kind of knock as if whoever was there wasn't quite sure they should be.

'The door's open.' I called, swinging my legs to the floor and straightening my tie. I had to look my best if this was business of any kind.

When she walked in my first guess was that she was Marcia Edwards' daughter. A second look, however, convinced me that she wasn't.

She was certainly the type you'd find in the fancy high-class joints uptown with half a dozen guys in monkey suits hanging around waiting to fill her glass with champagne — tall and elegant with all of the curves in the right places. But I couldn't figure her as being Charles Kenton's wife.

I guessed she was around thirty give or take a couple of years. She was definitely not the sort of woman who would associate with a private eye like Johnny Merak unless she was in very serious trouble.

She walked over to the chair in front of the desk and sat down crossing her legs in the way that told me she knew exactly how to handle men.

Looking straight at me, she said in a

low, husky voice, 'You're Johnny Merak, aren't you?'

'That's the name on the door,' I said. Dawn got up and moved over to her chair without saying a word. 'You got something on your mind?'

She nodded, her shoulder-length golden hair following every little movement. 'You wouldn't have a drink, would you? I know it's a little early in the day but — '

I could tell by the way she looked at my half empty cup of coffee that she wasn't thinking of that. I pulled open the drawer of my desk and took out the bottle of Scotch and a glass. Pouring a good measure into the glass, I slid it across the desk towards her. She took it and drank half of it in a single swallow.

Dawn gave her a funny look but kept her mouth shut, leaving me to do the talking.

Putting the glass down she said, 'I'd like to hire you, Mister Merak — a thousand dollar retainer and twice your usual expenses.' This time she stared hard at me over the rim of her glass. There was something in her eyes that told me she was not only deadly serious but she was also scared.

'First,' I said, 'I'd like to know exactly who it is I'd be working for.' I had the gut feeling I'd seen her someplace before but I couldn't remember exactly where.

'My name is Angela Cliveden.' She didn't smile as she gave me her name — in fact she hadn't smiled once since coming into the office. 'You may have seen me pictured in some of the glossy fashion magazines.'

Something clicked in my mind. I threw Dawn a quick glance as she held up one of the magazines she usually read when the place was quiet. Angela's face stared across the room at me from the front page.

'Of course,' I said hastily. 'But I have to tell you I'm already working on a pretty big case at the moment. Why should you need my help — and why me? Surely a dame like you could hire any private detective in L.A.'

'I suppose I could do that but I've asked around and my guess is that you're one of the best and you also know when to keep your mouth shut.'

What she said, and the way she said it, made it all sound intriguing but being a cautious guy I wanted to know exactly what I was letting myself in for. A lot of these high-flying dames also had links with the Mobs. Not that she would ever admit it, of course. I didn't particularly want to take on two different cases, both connected with the Organizations.

'I think someone is out to kill me,' she went on before I could ask anything more.

I guess my eyebrows went up half an inch because she continued, 'I'm perfectly serious, Mister Merak. And believe me, I'm not an hysterical woman who imagines these things.'

'No, of course not,' I said hurriedly. I noticed her glass was empty and poured more of the liquor into it.

She was silent for a while, twirling the glass in her finely manicured fingers. I noticed her hand was shaking in spite of the effort she made to control it. Maybe, I figured, she was wondering whether she was doing the right thing confiding in me.

Breaking the silence I said, 'Do you have any idea who this someone might be?'

She shook her head slowly. 'No. Just phone calls that started about a couple of weeks ago.'

'Man or woman?' I asked.

'Definitely a man,' she replied.

'So have you been to the cops?'

Her smile was bitter. 'They all said the same thing. All they could do was put a tap on my phone but so far they've done nothing. You're my last hope.' Her voice now had a pleading edge. 'Will you help me?'

'Never let it be said that Johnny Merak left a damsel in distress. I'll help you but there's a lot more I need to know.'

'You're a gentleman,' she said.

I grinned. 'I've been called a lot of names but nobody has ever called me that before. Can you come back around this time tomorrow?'

'I'll try.'

I gave her my business card. She gave it a brief glance and then slipped it into her bag.

Picking up her drink she finished it in one swallow and then fished inside the black-and-gold bag again. She took out a small envelope and handed it to me. 'One thousand dollars,' she said. Getting elegantly to her feet, she left, closing the door softly behind her.

Going to the window, I glanced down at the sidewalk. There was a silver limousine standing at the kerb. A few moments later, she appeared. Slipping behind the wheel, she pulled out into the stream of traffic and drove off.

'You really think a woman like that, with all the dough she's obviously got, could be in any danger, Johnny?'

Dawn was standing beside me, staring down at the street.

I shrugged. 'Maybe the guy she's going with, the one with the real money, is getting tired of her and wants her out of his life — permanently,' I told her. 'It sometimes happens that way.'

I tried to figure out what it was about this dame that intrigued me. I'd already guessed she hadn't told me everything. It was quite possible she had links with one of the organizations. Dames like that very seldom got to be where they were by their own efforts. Somewhere in the background was someone providing both the dough and the necessary connections for her.

Those tireless little mice were warning me that if this was the case, I should have stayed clear of Angela Cliveden. I already had one case that was going to take up a lot of my time, even with Dawn's help.

Maybe I was going to regret what I'd just done but Father Time has a nasty habit of not allowing you to go back and undo your mistakes.

I sent Dawn off to check on any close boyfriends Angela might have. While she was away I tried to concentrate on my first case. I poured myself a drink and attempted to list the most likely places where a small boy might be hidden.

By the time we were finished for the day, I wasn't much further on. There wasn't much on Angela Cliveden. She'd made a few enemies in the modelling business as she'd somehow clawed her way to the top. But I couldn't imagine any disgruntled competitor wanting to murder her.

That evening, I walked back to my apartment and let myself in. I'd only had a couple of drinks in the office and five minutes later I was sitting at the table with a bottle and glass in front of me. The warmth from the electric fire was slowly easing a little of the chill in my bones and I figured the whiskey would help with the rest.

I couldn't get the picture of Angela Cliveden out of my head. I'd known women before who were absolutely convinced someone was out to kill them but as far as I could remember it had never happened. So what was so different about this one?

It was something I couldn't figure out. Those little mice inside my head were telling me there were only two possibilities. Either her boyfriend was getting tired of her — or he had caught her cheating with someone else. Either way, her life could well be in danger of being snuffed out. I leaned back in my chair. Maybe, I thought, I'd get some answers in the morning.

Some time later I must have fallen asleep in the chair. I might have slept through until morning but a knocking on the door woke me at once. A quick glance at my watch told me it was a little after two thirty. Jerking forward in the chair, I tried to get my thoughts into some kind of order.

I couldn't think of anyone who would come calling at that ungodly hour of the morning but there was something about that knock that told me I'd better answer it quickly. Unlocking the door, I opened it to reveal two bruisers standing on my doorstep.

They pushed their way inside without a word. I recognized their type at once. Dark, almost identical suits, hard eyes and faces. They were the kind of men who did the dirty work for the big boys; men who asked no questions and obeyed orders. One of them closed the door; then motioned me towards the bed. My gun lay on the small table beside it but I knew better than to make a grab for it.

They stood there for a minute just

staring at me like Tweedledum and Tweedledee. I'd had dealings with such men before; men who killed just for the sheer hell of it.

Somehow I found my voice. 'Hey,' I said. I took a step towards the table but the slightly bigger of the two moved quickly. My wrist was caught in a grip like a vise while his other hand grabbed my gun and slipped it into his pocket.

'All right,' I said hoarsely. 'Just what is this?'

'Get your coat on, Merak. Someone wants to see you — right now.'

'Now just a minute,' I began. My first thought was that Enrico Manzelli had sent these bruisers. He was the big man as far as the L.A. Underworld was concerned — the man who gave all of the orders to the various organizations. And any command he gave was obeyed instantly and without question.

'If Manzelli wants to see me he usually lets me know,' I said, hoping that the fact that I'd had previous dealings with the big boss might go in my favour with these guys. Such men as these two had been known to rough you up a little if you didn't do as they said.

'Now what makes you think it's Manzelli who's asking for you, Merak?' muttered the smaller of the two. He stood watching me as I shrugged into my jacket and I noticed his right hand never strayed far from his pocket. No doubt there was a gun nestling there ready to be used if I gave any sign of making trouble.

'No particular reason,' I said. 'Just that I've done him a couple of favours in the past.'

'Well for your information it ain't Manzelli,' he growled, 'and the guy you're going to see won't be doing you any favours.' He uttered a harsh laugh like a hyena that had just caught its prey.

One of them took out a gun and pushed it hard between my shoulder blades as I went outside and locked the door behind me. It was a purely reflex gesture. The way things were going I didn't know whether or not I would be coming back.

There was a big black limousine waiting at the sidewalk. One of the bruisers thrust me into the back and crushed in beside me. The other one got in the front beside the guy behind the wheel.

There was scarcely any traffic at that time of the morning. A couple of late-night cabs cruised past but that was all. Pretty soon I realized we were not heading out of town towards the open country where Manzelli lived. Instead, we were driving towards the plush side of the city.

Leaving the freeway we passed through part of downtown L.A. — an area dotted with neon-lit nightclubs, all-night bars and sleazy gambling joints. Here there were more people around; the anonymous, shadowy night populations. Faces you scarcely ever saw in the daytime; faces that saw very little sunlight.

Leaning forward a little, I asked, 'Just where are we going?'

The guy next to me muttered, 'Sit back. Merak, you'll find out soon enough.'

I sat back, knowing I'd get nothing more out of them. Through the window, I saw that we were now entering the more classy part of the city. Here there were the places where movie stars lived beside the top men in the mobs. Not that they knew it, of course. The latter were extremely careful to hide their true backgrounds.

Thirty yards ahead, on the right, stood as couple of big metal gates. They were open and I guessed this was our destination. Where these guys were concerned security was a top priority and I knew those gates would never have been open unless we were expected.

There was the crunch of gravel on the wheels as we drove in and parked at the front of the imposing entrance. My companion got out and motioned to me to do the same.

I did as I was told. Now I was inside those gates I had no choice if I wanted to remain healthy. But I still couldn't figure out who it could be who wanted me in such a hurry.

Inside the house I was led along a wide corridor. The walls were bare, but the wallpaper was nice, and I reckoned that whoever owned this place didn't go in for collecting original paintings like some of the top men in the organizations.

There was a door at the end of the corridor and one of my companions gave a polite knock before pushing it open. He said something to someone inside and then thrust me forward.

I recognized the guy seated behind the huge desk at once. Tony Minello. He was one of the top men in the organization run by Sam Rizzio. I knew a little about him, that he'd come over from Sicily some ten years before and joined up with the big man at the time — Carlos Galecchi.

Carlos had been murdered a year before and I happened to be the one who had pinned his killing on Lieutenant Donovan from the local precinct. Since that time my relations with Rizzio were cordial, at least on the surface.

He got to his feet as I entered, tall and thin with a hard face that would have cracked if he'd ever smiled. His dark eyes were the kind that drilled right through you so you felt his gaze scratching away at the back of your skull.

He walked around the side of the desk

and looked me up and down for a moment. 'Are you this private dick, Johnny Merak?' he asked finally. There was the trace of an Italian accent to his voice but it wasn't melodious like the opera singers. Rather it was like a rasp grinding on metal.

I nodded, wondering what was coming next. I could see there was something on his mind but I couldn't guess what it was — anger, frustration or maybe some deeply held resentment.

Turning, he picked up something from the desk and held it out to me. 'Is this yours?' There was a definite note of menace in his tone now.

I glanced at it. It was my business card with my name and phone number on it.

'Yes, it's mine,' I replied. 'Where did you get it?'

He hesitated and then jerked his thumb towards the far door. 'Bring him along,' he said to the two guys standing just behind me.

Both of them grabbed my arms and hustled me towards the door with Minello leading the way. They took me up two flights of stairs. There was a half open door at the top and lights on inside the room. It was a bedroom, a woman's room. There was the faint scent of perfume in the air, decorative furniture of the highest quality. Near the far wall stood a four-poster bed and on the floor beside it lay a woman's body with one arm flung out on the rich green carpet as if trying to clutch at something just out of reach.

One glance was enough to tell me she was dead and I didn't need a second look to tell me who she was — Angela Cliveden!

Minello swung on me. I could see he'd taken this pretty badly and it didn't take the intelligence of an Archbishop to tell me there had been something between him and Angela.

Thrusting his face up to mine, his thin lips drawn back across his teeth, Minello snarled, 'Now you're going to tell me how your card got into Angela's handbag and it had better be good or you won't live to see the daylight.'

I knew it was no idle threat. Swallowing

hard, I said, 'I gave it to her.'

'You gave it to her? When?'

'Late yesterday morning. She came into my office and told me there'd been threats against her life. She hired me to find out who wanted her dead and gave me a thousand dollar retainer for my services.'

The expression on Minello's face was one I couldn't analyze. Shock, anger, utter disbelief at what had happened — it could have been anything. Finally, he said, 'Well, you certainly didn't do a good job of helping her, did you?'

For a moment, I thought he was going to accuse me of her murder. 'Hell,' I said sharply, 'I only met her once for a few minutes. She said she'd come to my office again. There were a few more questions I wanted to ask her. There was no way I could even guess anything like this might happen.'

Giving me no reply, he walked away and stood looking down at the body. Then he bent and made to turn her over.

'I wouldn't touch her if I were you,' I said quickly. 'The cops will want to see everything just as it is.'

Whatever emotion filled his mind at that moment my warning seemed to penetrate it. Straightening slowly, he stared hard at me. 'I haven't called the police yet. I wanted to hear what you had to say first.'

Minello's lips were clamped together into a thin line. It was clear he still hadn't made up his mind about me. My position was still highly precarious. One wrong word, one move he didn't like, and I'd be taking a dip in the sea — all the way to the bottom.

He turned swiftly to one of the men standing like guard dogs beside me. 'Get on the phone to the photo agency. See if Angela had an appointment with anyone yesterday morning.'

The guy glanced swiftly at his wristwatch. 'That place won't be open now, boss.'

'I don't give a damn about that,' Minello was almost shouting the words. 'Get the number of the guy who runs the agency and wake him up. The number will be in Angela's diary on the desk yonder.'

The big guy went over to the desk, checked through the pages and then dialled a number.

I was on the point of warning him that his prints would now be all over the phone and the diary but I thought — What the hell! All I wanted to do was get out of this place with a whole skin.

The guy spoke for a couple of minutes and after a few moments he nodded his head and put the receiver down.

'Well?' Minello demanded.

'He seems to be telling the truth, Tony. She did say she's be out of the studio for an hour and she was going to see this guy, Merak.'

Minello's face changed a little at that. I could still feel the chill of sweat on my back but for the time being it seemed the heat was off.

I expected him to tell the two bruisers to take me back to my apartment. Instead, he said thinly, 'That thousand dollars Angela gave you, Merak, I expect you to earn it. Someone did this and I want you to find out who it was. You just give me the name and the proof and I'll do the rest.'

'Aren't you going to phone the cops?'

He nodded. 'I'm going to call them now. I want you to stay until they arrive, take a look around. If you've got any questions ask them before the police get here. Have you got that?' He threw a quick glance at my business card still in his hand. Then he gave it back to me. 'No need for the cops to find this,' he said meaningfully.

'Thanks,' I said. 'Just one thing first before I start.'

'What's that?'

'Anything I find — do I tell you first or the cops?'

'You tell me.'

I stepped forward and went down on one knee to get a closer look at the body and it was then I noticed something between the carpet and her hand.

'What is it?' Minello asked sharply.

'I'm not sure.' I glanced up. 'See if you can find a pair of eyebrow tweezers on the table yonder. Whatever it is, I don't want my prints all over it.'

After a couple of minutes, one of the guys came back and handed me the tweezers. I gently lifted the object from the carpet. It was a small square of paper. A curious symbol had been drawn on it with black ink.

Minello glanced at it over my shoulder. 'You got any idea what it means?' he asked.

I shook my head. 'Never seen anything like it before,' I told him. 'One thing I am sure of, however. The killer left this for either you — or the cops — to find.'

'You figure it's important then that the cops should have it?'

'I guess you could call that a vital clue. We'd better put it back where it was but first I'd like to make a copy of it. I know someone who might know what it, represents.' I took out my pen and cigarette pack and drew the symbol on the back before putting the piece of paper back on the carpet.

Then, after only a momentary hesitation, Minello walked across the room and phoned the cops.

2

Ten minutes later a siren wailed outside like a tormented soul in Purgatory. It stopped in front of the house. A few minutes later, four cops came into the room. Two I didn't know. The others were Lieutenant O'Leary and Sergeant Kolowinski of the Homicide Squad.

O'Leary threw me a funny look. 'You're the last person I expected to see here, Merak,' he said thinly. 'I've never known you to get onto a case so quickly — unless you're somehow mixed up in this.'

'I asked Mister Merak to come over here, Lieutenant,' Minello butted in.

'And why would you do that? Is he working on a case for you?'

'He's agreed to find out for me who killed Angela.'

'Maybe he has but this is a homicide case.' O'Leary's voice was so hard you could have struck sparks off it. 'Whatever he does for you, he'd better keep out of my hair.'

'You're swimming in dangerous waters now, Johnny.' Kolowinski spoke up for the first time. 'There are plenty of sharks around and some have bigger teeth than others.' He was bending over the body. I knew he was just giving me a friendly warning and I hoped I'd live long enough to appreciate it.

Glancing round, he spoke directly to O'Leary. 'Take a look at this, Lieutenant.' He pointed to the small square of paper.

Before he could pick it up there was a knock on the door and a small guy walked in. I guessed he was the doctor. He waited while one of the other cops took a number of pictures of the body before kneeling down and giving her the once-over.

Finally, he said, 'A single stab wound to the heart. There doesn't appear to be any other marks on her. I'd say she's been dead not more than a couple of hours but I can't tell you exactly until I've made a post-mortem.'

'Any sign of a struggle?' O'Leary asked.

'None that I can see.'

O'Leary nodded, satisfied. 'Then I guess she either knew her assailant pretty well or it was someone she reckoned didn't represent any threat to her.'

'And no sign of the murder weapon either.' Kolowinski remarked dryly. He swung his gaze on Minello. 'Did you take it?'

'You can't pin this one on me.' Minello almost snarled the words. 'This is exactly how I found her not more than an hour ago. I've got plenty of witnesses to back me up on that.'

'I'll bet you have.' The Lieutenant's tone was only slightly less direct than Minello's. 'I know your kind. You'd send your own mother to the chair to clear yourself.'

For a moment I thought Minello was about to reach for the gun he always carried under his left arm. If looks could kill, O'Leary would've dropped dead at my feet. Then he managed to pull himself together. 'I don't give a damn what you think, O'Leary, but if I find whoever did this there won't be any trial. You'll find them at the bottom of the river — if you're lucky.'

O'Leary said nothing. He turned to the guy who had been taking the photographs. 'You finished here, Lacey?'

'All finished, Lieutenant. She's all yours.'

Bending, O'Leary picked up the piece of paper by one corner and scrutinized it closely with a puzzled expression on his hard features.

He showed it around. 'Any of you knows what this is supposed to mean? Some gang sign, perhaps.'

When everyone shook their heads, he shrugged and placed it carefully in a plastic bag. Turning to me, he said sharply, 'I reckon you can go, Merak. This is a police homicide case and I don't want you sticking your nose in. You got that?'

'Sure thing, Lieutenant.' I looked across at Minello.

He nodded. 'Carlos here will take you back,' he said. 'And don't forget what I told you.'

'I won't.' I knew O'Leary was watching me like a dog staring at a bone, trying to figure out what that remark meant.

Then the tall guy had me by the arm and was leading me out of the room and along the corridor to the front door. The night air smelled good, and fresh, after the atmosphere in that room. Those little mice had started running around inside my head again but I did my best to ignore them during the ride back to my apartment.

There were a lot of questions that needed answers but at the moment I didn't have any. Had Angela been killed because she'd spoken to me? Was there something she knew that had to stay hidden? And what was that symbol on the piece of paper? I didn't doubt that the killer had left it there for a purpose.

Carlos let me off just outside my apartment. I watched the twin tail-lights until they vanished around a corner and then went in. The next morning I was seated in my swivel chair with my legs on the desk. Dawn was making coffee while I told her what had happened the previous night. Bringing over my drink, she shifted a few papers and set the mug down in front of me.

'Do you reckon this Angela woman knew her killer?' she asked, returning to her chair.

I thought about that for a minute before answering. 'Could be,' I said finally. 'There was no sign of a struggle or a break-in and I'm sure it wasn't a robbery that went wrong. Nothing seemed to have been taken and there were plenty of expensive jewels lying around all in their proper place.

'There was one funny thing, though, and I'm hoping you can help me with it.' I dug into my jacket pocket and pulled out my cigarette pack. Handing it to her, I went on, 'There was a piece of paper just beside the body with that symbol on it in black ink. It's quite clear the killer left it there. Do you know what it is?'

Dawn glanced at it, turning the packet slowly in her fingers. For a moment she looked just as puzzled as O'Leary and the others had been. Then she nodded. 'Sure, I recognize it. It's alpha.'

'Alpha? What the hell's that?'

Dawn grinned. 'If you'd stayed with your education, Johnny, you might have known. It's the first letter of the Greek alphabet.'

I still couldn't see what this had to do with Angela's murder.

Noticing the puzzled expression on my face, Dawn went on, 'I think that if this is, indeed, the killer's calling card, this symbol has some real significance.'

'In what way?' I asked, trying to figure out what she was getting at.

'Literally it means the first — or the beginning. I don't want to scare you, Johnny, but I'd say this isn't a one-off murder. It's the first of many.'

I turned that over in my mind and I didn't like the conclusion I was coming to. 'Then, if you're right, it's obvious what the killer is telling us. He's embarked on some kind of vendetta against Rizzio and Minello. But why Angela — why not kill Minello? I wonder what O'Leary will think if he — '

I broke off sharply at the sound of heavy footsteps in the corridor outside. There was a hard knock on the door and before I could call out it was pushed open and two guys came in.

As I'd figured, it was O'Leary, closely followed by Sergeant Kolowinski. The look on the Lieutenant's face told me he wanted some answers and if he didn't get them I was wasting his time and that was something he didn't like.

He took something from his inside pocket and tossed it onto the desk. 'Guess you haven't read the paper today,' he grated. His voice was like metal pulverizing granite. 'It made the front page.'

Opening the newspaper, I glanced at the front. The headline jumped out at me, hitting me right between the eyes.

L.A. FASHION MODEL SLAIN.

I didn't have to read much of the story. I guess I knew about as much as he did.

Dawn had got to her feet and was staring over my shoulder at the newspaper. I said, 'It didn't take them long to get this story.'

O'Leary placed his ham-sized fists on the desk and leaned forward until his face almost touched mine. 'Did you give them any of this, probably to make a little cheap publicity for yourself? I heard what Minello said last night as you were leaving and my guess is that you're somehow tied in with him.'

'All right, Lieutenant, I'll tell you. My beauty sleep was rudely disturbed last night by two of Minello's bruisers. They hauled me off to see him. I guess I managed to convince him I had nothing to do with her murder although he knew she'd been to see me.'

'How did he know that?'

'He found my card in her handbag. When he knew I was on the level, he asked me to find out who killed her. Like it or not, that's my job.'

'Once a mobster, always a mobster.' He almost snarled the words at me, possibly hoping to provoke me into saying something I didn't want to.

'Not at all, but I'll take the devil's dough if it helps to pay the rent.'

He didn't like that and switched the subject. 'There are some questions, Merak, and you'd better give me some straight answers. You seem to be the last person to see Angela Cliveden alive.'

I shook my head. 'You're wrong, Lieutenant. Someone saw her after me.'

'Oh yeah. Who?'

'The killer,' I said evenly. 'Okay, so she came to ask for my help.'

'Care to tell me what you talked about and don't give me any malarky about it was the first time you'd met her, she somehow reminded you of your mother, and it was because she figured you're the best dick in L.A. Dames like that don't mix with your kind.'

'I guess they don't mix with your kind either.' I took out a cigarette and lit it, trying to appear casual. 'She wanted to hire my services,' I said through the smoke. 'In case you hadn't noticed the sign on the door, that's my business — private detective.'

O'Leary pushed back his hat. 'So what did you talk about?'

'That,' I said, 'comes under client confidentiality.'

I must have been getting to him for he slammed down a fist like the hind leg of a mule on the desk. 'I don't give a damn about client confidentiality, Merak. And in case you hadn't noticed, your client is dead. This is a homicide case and you can either answer my questions here or down at the precinct.' The expression on his face implied that he would prefer it to be the latter.

'All right,' I said, blowing a cloud of blue smoke into the air. 'I'll tell you. She believed someone wanted to see her laid out in the morgue.'

'Obviously what she said wasn't very far from the truth.' Kolowinski spoke up for the first time. He was standing next the door, an odd expression on his face.

'Did you kill her?' O'Leary snapped.

I stared at him. 'You've got a very suspicious mind, Lieutenant.' I said. 'What motive would I have for killing a client? Besides, like I said, I'd never met her before yesterday. I didn't even know where she lived.'

O'Leary shrugged. 'I've only got your word for that, Merak. For all I know she had something on you, maybe from the old Mob days, and was trying her hand at blackmail. I've known it happen.'

I got to my feet. 'Listen. All I know is

that this dame came to see me, said someone was out to murder her, and gave me a thousand dollar retainer. Dawn was here at the time. If you reckon you can pin this killing on me, you'd better arrest me now.'

He chewed that over for a full minute. Then he muttered, 'I guess I'll leave that until I've got more evidence. But don't leave town. There are more questions I want to ask you.'

'You know where to find me.'

He turned and made for the door.

As he reached it, I added, 'There's one thing you should know.'

Without turning, he asked in a low, menacing tone, 'And what's that, Merak?'

'I don't know who killed her but I sure intend to find out. I guess I owe her that much.'

He spun round so quickly he almost fell against Kolowinski. 'That's your affair, I suppose — yours and Minello's. But if you get under my feet I'll have your licence taken away so fast you won't have time to spit. You got that?'

'I've got it,' I replied.

He went out with Kolowinski following him like a faithful dog. The door slammed behind them.

My coffee was cold so Dawn made some more. Over her shoulder, she said, 'I think you've made an enemy of the Lieutenant, Johnny. Was that wise?'

'Damnit, Dawn! He practically accused me of murdering her.'

'So what do you intend to do now?'

I made up my mind at once. 'I've got to get as much background information as I can on Angela Cliveden. That's the only lead I've got at the moment. I want you to find out details of everyone she worked with on these magazines. Also any friends she had.' Those little mice careering around inside my head were performing cartwheels. They were telling me that if Angela had been dating Tony Minello, it was likely that he'd also been helping with her career. I might be putting my head on the chopping block. These guys didn't like anyone probing into their private lives too much and even though he'd asked me to find her killer, he wouldn't want me putting my nose in too far.

Before turning legit I'd worked with the Underworld and knew their methods well enough. I knew what happened to guys who started poking around. They ended up in some dark alley looking up at the stars but not seeing them — or they simply disappeared and nobody asked any questions.

There was, however, something else on my mind. I reached for the phone on the desk and dialled Minello's number. Some other guy answered but when I gave my name he put me through to Minello right away.

'Have you got something for me, Merak?' he asked.

'Nothing much at the moment,' I replied, 'but there is one thing I reckon you'd like to know.'

'What's that?'

'That piece of paper we found near Angela's body; the one with the curious symbol on it.'

'I remember. What of it?'

'Seems my secretary knows a little more than we do. According to her it's the Greek letter alpha, the first letter of the alphabet. Her guess is, and I agree with her on this, that this isn't just a one-off murder. There are going to be more.'

There was a pause while he thought that over. Then he snapped, 'If that's the case, the sooner you find out who this killer is and give me that information, the better.' He slammed the phone down.

Dawn got up from her chair. 'I'll try to find out as much as I can on who Angela was working with and also if there was anything serious between her and Minello.'

'In the meantime, I'll — ' I began.

I broke off in mid-sentence as the phone shrilled. I figured it might be O'Leary but it wasn't. The voice on the other end of the line had all the friendliness of a desert rattler. 'Someone wants to speak to you, Merak. Now! Be outside your office in five minutes.'

'And if I'm not.'

'Then you can kiss tomorrow goodbye.'

'Who is this?' I asked — but I was speaking to a dead line. I knew instinctively who had given this ultimatum. Enrico

Manzelli, the man who gave all the orders in L.A. I had met him face to face only once before. It was an experience I'd no wish to repeat. But when Manzelli gave an order everyone from the hoodlum on the street to the top politician jumped. No one said no to Enrico.

Dawn looked at me across the desk. Her voice trembled a little as she said, 'I gather that wasn't a friend of yours.'

'I doubt if even his mother was a friend of his.'

She guessed it right away. 'Manzelli. But what does he want with you?'

'That is something you don't find out unless you're staring down the barrel of a gun or looking up into his baby-blue eyes,' I told her. 'Seems there'll be a car waiting outside in five minutes.'

'But you're not in the Mob now, Johnny. You don't have to jump every time he snaps his fingers.'

'I reckon it's the lesser of two evils — see what he wants or have his hoods on my tail.' I picked up my hat and jammed it on my head. 'Hold the fort until I get back.'

'If you get back.' The way she said it, it was either a prayer or a statement of fact.

I went down to the sidewalk feeling as if I were being hung out to dry. Manzelli never sent for anyone unless it was important. He was the one guy who knew everything that happened in L.A. almost before it took place. He gave an order for someone to be rubbed out and a very short time later the guy dropped dead from lead poisoning.

Exactly on time, a long black limousine detached itself from the traffic and slid to the kerb as smoothly as if it were on ice. The rear door popped open and a big guy got out. He jerked a thumb and I got inside. I leaned back and tried to look unconcerned. I attempted to ignore those little mice running around inside my head. They were telling me I was emulating Daniel, going into the lions' den and unlike the last time I had seen Manzelli, this time I might not enjoy a ride back into town.

Neither the driver nor my companion spoke during the entire journey. Either they were the strong, silent type or they'd been told to keep their mouths shut. Knowing Manzelli, I figured the latter was the more probable. Half an hour later we drove up to the rear of the large house that stood alone in the country, miles from anywhere as if hiding away from the outside world.

The last time I'd been here it had been dark. Now I got an eyeful of the place as the big guy hustled me round to the rear door. This was something straight out of Hollywood. It stood there in the middle of nothing like the centre of a spider's web with Enrico Manzelli as the spider. Invisible strands spread out from here to encompass the whole of L.A.

Few people had seen Manzelli but the orders he gave touched almost everyone in town.

The room into which I saw shown was dark with only a single dim lamp on the highly polished desk. It was the same room I'd been in once before. Unlike most of the men who ran the various organizations in L.A., Manzelli preferred to live anonymously in the shadows.

The big guy pointed towards the chair

in front of the desk. I sat down and stared straight ahead at the large chair across from me. I felt like someone waiting to walk along death row to the electric chair.

Five minutes dragged by so slowly it was as if Father Time had them on a tight rein. The silence began to eat at my nerves like acid.

Then a door to my left opened, so quietly it was like a shadow moving along the wall. The faint light that showed was immediately blotted out by the enormous bulk of Manzetti. He walked — or rather waddled — to the desk and somehow succeeded in lowering himself into the chair. Manzelli didn't move fast but then he didn't have to move for anyone.

His face resembled those of the American presidents on Mount Rushmore — not a muscle twitched and his eyes, almost hidden by flesh, bored into me as though searching my soul.

Placing his hands on the desk, he said, 'Much as I dislike doing business with men like you, Merak, there are unfortunately times when I have no choice.'

He was well aware, of course, that I had

once been a minor cog in the machinery of the Mob, and of my present links with the FBI. Why I was still alive was something I couldn't figure out. Either I was born to lead a charmed life — or at the moment my name wasn't on St. Peter's list. Certainly, as far as Manzelli was concerned, it wasn't out of the kindness of his heart. Maybe he thought I didn't count for anything. His next words confirmed this.

'You realize, of course, that when you defected from the Organization, I could have had you killed just by snapping my fingers.'

'Then why didn't you?' I knew it wasn't the right question to ask a guy like him.

He was silent for a full minute as if, like himself, thoughts moved slowly through his mind.

Finally, he said, 'Perhaps I foresaw there might come a time when you could still be useful to me. Then, you were only a small part of the Organization — a very small part indeed.'

Clasping his hands together in front of him, he continued, 'There is something you can do for me, just a small thing — someone is attempting to start a full-scale gang war in my territory. You are already aware, of course, of this unfortunate murder.'

I nodded. 'I met Angela Cliveden yesterday. She asked for my help.'

Now it was his turn to nod. 'I know that already. Like Tony Minello, I also want you to find out who killed this woman — and I want it done quickly.'

I could see that Minello would be peeved at his girlfriend being bumped off but I couldn't work out why the murder of a model was of such great importance to Manzelli.

Even in the dim light, he must have noticed the expression on my face for he leaned forward over the desk and went on, 'I see you are puzzled, Mister Merak.'

'The idea that something is very wrong had crossed my mind,' I replied.

'She was Antonio Minello's girlfriend. Perhaps you've heard of him.'

'Sure.' I nodded. 'I've already met him. He's one of the top men in Sam Rizzio's outfit. He's already asked me to find her killer.'

'You are quite correct, of course, about him being one of the top men. He's been quite useful to me in the past and my guess is that he won't be very pleased about her murder. There will undoubtedly be some form of retaliation. Already I have heard whispers that the blame for this killing will be laid at the door of someone in Malloy's organization.'

That news shook me. Malloy and Rizzio had been rivals for a long time but so far — due no doubt to Manzelli — an uneasy truce had existed between them. But if word got around that someone in Malloy's mob had murdered Minello's girlfriend a full-scale gang war was liable to break out. I could fully understand Manzelli not wanting this to happen.

'Do you reckon one of Malloy's men did this?' I asked.

Manzelli sat there as if carved from granite. I could almost hear the thoughts drifting through that cold calculating mind of his.

His next words, however, took me

completely by surprise. 'No, I don't. That is why I brought you here. I'm sure this matter goes much deeper than that. Nothing is what it appears to be. My belief is that there is someone in the shadows, someone who is determined to set Rizzio and Malloy at each other's throats. I'm sure you can see my position. That is something I must prevent at all costs — and quickly.'

You mean something Johnny Merak has to prevent. I didn't say the words out aloud. That would have been close to suicidal.

He took something from his left hand. 'I fully appreciate the — shall we say difficulties? — you may come up against in this matter. Anyone who probes into the various organizations does not usually live long enough to tell me anything. You may need some kind of protection.' He slid the object across the desk towards me. 'Show this to any member of the organizations and they'll know you're working solely for me.'

I picked it up and stared at it in what little light there was in the room. It was a large ring with a deep red stone set in a gold oval. There was a design inlaid in gold in the centre of the stone. I placed it on the middle finger of my left hand where it hung loosely, gleaming faintly in the light. Inwardly, I hoped it wouldn't have the opposite effect and make me a sitting target.

Manzetti pushed himself awkwardly out of his chair. 'That will be all for the time being, Mister Merak.'

I waited until he'd gone before getting up and turning to the bruiser standing motionless at the door. He spun round without a word and led me along the corridor and outside to where the car was waiting.

He was watching me closely out of the corner of his eye, possibly wondering why Manzelli had entrusted me with this job and not him. He evidently never realized that there were times when you settled things with guns — and other times when you needed brains.

The journey back was as uneventful as sitting and watching grass grow. The limousine slid smoothly to a stop at the sidewalk and I got out and went up to my office. Dawn wasn't in but she came in twenty minutes and a couple of cigarettes later.

'Was it Manzelli who wanted to see you, Johnny?'

'Yeah.' I nodded. 'It was the big boss himself.'

'And what did he want?' She placed the papers she was carrying onto her desk; then turned to look directly at me.

'Just as I figured. He wants me to find out who murdered Angela and he wants it done yesterday before a full scale gang war breaks out.'

She walked over and sat on the edge of the desk, swinging her shapely legs slightly. It was then she noticed the ring on my finger.

Before she could ask the obvious question, I said, 'It's Manzelli's ring. Just in case I should run into any serious trouble with anyone in the organizations, they'll know I'm working for him.'

'And you think that will stop you getting a bullet in the back or dumped somewhere out at sea?'

'It might. If I go through with this case, I reckon it's the only thing that will.'

She stood up. 'You're a goddamn fool, Johnny. I've said it before a hundred times and I'm saying it again. Why don't you stick to what you're good at — tracking down missing people — and leave these gang killings to the police? Don't forget you still have this other case on the files, looking for Mrs. Edwards' grandson. Even though the Mobs may be mixed up in it, I reckon it'll be less dangerous than what Manzelli wants you to do.'

Staring down at the ring on my finger, I replied, 'I guess I'm one of those guys who's always followed by trouble — big-time.'

She made an exasperated sound. 'One of these days trouble like this is going to be the end of you.'

I could have sworn there were tears in her eyes as she turned sharply and changed the subject, 'You want a coffee?'

'I could sure use one,' I said. I took the ring from my finger and slipped it into my pocket. There seemed no sense in showing that around unless I had to. 'But first there's something I have to do. I've already told Minello about that symbol. I think I'd better let O'Leary know unless he's figured it out already.'

I picked up the phone and dialled the local precinct. The desk sergeant answered and put me through.

'O'Leary.' His voice was hard, like an iron bar. 'Have you got something for me, Merak? If not, don't waste my time. I've got Minello breathing down my neck.'

'Have you got anything yet on that piece of paper?'

'No, why?'

'My secretary recognized it right away. It's the first letter of the Greek alphabet. The way I see it the killer is telling us he intends to strike again.'

There was a long pause. I could visualize him sitting at his desk wondering if I had somehow hit the truth or was just winding him up. Finally, he grated, 'Is that all?'

'At the moment, yes.'

'Well, as far as I'm concerned this is most likely a mob slaying and I deal only in fact, not theories and suppositions. Right now, I've got enough on my hands. Now, unless you're deliberately keeping something from me, stay out of my hair.'

The line went dead. Replacing the receiver, I sat back and sipped the coffee Dawn placed in front of me. I knew I was keeping something from O'Leary but I had no intention of telling him of my talk with Manzelli. That would be close to suicidal and I might even find myself as murder suspect number one.

3

The Comero was a small Italian restaurant near the south end of town. Its usual clientele didn't include the rich and famous from Hollywood. But then it didn't entertain the down-and-outs or many of the night people who tended to frequent the all night bars either.

Dawn and I found a table in one corner away from the main door when it was possible to scrutinize anyone coming in or going out. My main reason for going there, apart from the food and wine that were excellent, was because several of the top men in the Malloy Organization used it as a meeting place. Sometimes Joe Malloy himself came and he was the guy I wanted to see.

Dawn was there just to keep me out of trouble.

That wasn't always the case, of course. Some of these guys were not averse to slapping a woman down, especially if the alcohol got to their brains. I did, however, have my own back up if things got really nasty — the .38 nestling in its shoulder holster and that ring Manzelli had given me.

Eugene, the owner, generally did his best to limit the number of guns entering the place. He let me in, however, without frisking me. Maybe he figured that being with a high-class dame like Dawn, and not a member of the Mobs, I wasn't likely to be carrying any artillery with me.

The restaurant was quite crowded even at that early hour of the evening. We placed our order and then I sat back and surveyed the customers. I immediately recognized two guys, sitting with their wives or secretaries. They occupied different tables but both were high fliers from City Hall — the kind of guys who could do big favours provided you got to know them well enough and had the right kind of dough.

'You expecting to see anyone in particular, Johnny?' Dawn leaned across the table and spoke in a low voice.

'I was hoping that either Joe Malloy or

'some of his top men might be in.'

'Malloy?' I could see she was suddenly getting nervous. 'Don't tell me you came here to meet him? He's a killer, Johnny, probably worse than Rizzio.'

'You don't have to tell me that, Dawn. I've had dealings with him before. But if I'm to get anywhere with this investigation, there are a few questions I have to ask him.'

Our order came and Dawn waited until the waiter had moved away before asking, 'What sort of questions?' She looked across at me, her spoon poised halfway to her lips.

'Like whether it was any of his men who killed Minello's girlfriend,' I said.

Dawn wiped her mouth with her napkin. She said dryly, 'Don't you think that would be a fool question to ask a man like him? Even if it were some member of his organization, he'd deny it. And for anyone poking his nose into his business, that would be the least he'd do.'

'Meaning?'

'You know what I mean, Johnny. Pretty soon, they'd find you at the bottom of the river someplace or in a back alley with your skull bashed in. Why don't you — ?'

She broke off hastily as I put my finger to my lips. Three men had come into the restaurant. Two I didn't know. The third was Joe Malloy. I watched the trio closely as they were shown to a table on the far side of the room. I noticed how the chairs were arranged so they would all sit with their backs to the wall where they could see anyone coming through the door. Either they were expecting trouble or intended making some of their own. Whichever way it was going to turn out I knew I had to have a word with Malloy before the tables started flying in all directions.

Malloy made to sit down but then turned and walked over to one of the guys I'd noticed earlier. Placing a hand on his shoulder, Malloy bent and whispered something in the guy's ear. Before straightening up, he slipped an envelope from his inside pocket and slid it into the other fellow's jacket pocket.

Dawn had also noticed. 'Evidently a pay-off,' I told her quietly. 'It would seem

Malloy has some big business deals on the side.'

I waited until Malloy went back to his table and slid into the chair between the two bruisers he'd brought with him.

'Excuse me for a couple of minutes, Dawn,' I said, getting to my feet.

She started to say something and put out a hand to clutch my sleeve. I knew what she was thinking — that I was walking straight into trouble. It was very likely she was right.

I saw Malloy glance up as I approached his table and both of his minders immediately placed their right hands inside their jackets. They might have been reaching for a pack of cigarettes but somehow I didn't think so.

Malloy was a little guy with eyes like gimlets that bored right into you, stripping your soul naked. He'd have made a good agent for the Devil, picking out the right customers. His suit was immaculate and I reckoned the bright emerald green tie he wore was in honour of his country of origin.

His thin lips twisted into a hard line

and I knew he'd recognized me. For a moment, he said nothing but continued to stare at me like a snake about to strike. Then he smiled but it wasn't a nice smile.

'Johnny Merak,' he said thinly. 'Well, well. I hear you're a private dick now and more to the point you're still in cahoots with Sam Rizzio. Is that true?'

'He's asked me to take on a case for him,' I admitted. With those eyes boring into me it was difficult to lie.

'A pity about Minello's girl.'

'Yeah, a great pity,' I said. I came straight to the point. 'Did you have anything to do with her murder, Joe?'

His eyes narrowed down but beyond that he showed no emotion whatsoever. I'd expected him to lean across the table and try to put one on my jaw.

Instead, he merely shrugged. 'Why should I want her killed? She meant nothing to me. I've never even met the dame.'

'But maybe you figured that this might start a gang war. You've always wanted a slice of Rizzio's territory. If Minello figures you're responsible and retaliates in some way it would give you an excuse to start something.'

Malloy placed the tips of his fingers together and sat back, not once taking his eyes off me. 'You're beginning to bore me, Merak, with your accusations. I don't like that. I suggest you go back to your lady friend and stay out of my business, otherwise things could get mighty unpleasant.'

'Unpleasant for you, perhaps. If Manzelli gets to hear about any little scheme you have in mind, he might not be too pleased.'

This time I'd hit a raw nerve. There was a purple vein standing out in his forehead as he jumped to his feet. 'Now you have gone too far,' he hissed venomously. 'You're a dead man, Merak.' He swung his gaze to the two bruisers on either side of him. 'Take him outside and see that he doesn't come back.'

'I wouldn't do that, Malloy.' I moved my right hand very slowly towards my pocket, 'until you've seen this. I think you'll recognize it.'

I pulled out Manzelli's ring and held it out in the palm of my hand. It gleamed a

71

dark red in the light of the crystal chandelier overhead.

Malloy looked as if he had been kicked in the face by a mule. He sank back into his chair. The two guys beside him removed their hands from inside their jackets. Neither of them held a gun.

'Where did you get that?' Malloy's voice was a hoarse whisper.

'Where do you think I got it?' I replied. I knew I'd now got his undivided attention. 'It was given to me by Manzelli.'

'You're working for him?'

'That's right.' I put it back into my pocket and straightened. 'I'm not interested in any crooked deal you may have made with that guy back there. Right now, I'm interested in only one thing. Did you or any of your boys murder that girl?'

Malloy shook his head. 'I had no part in it,' he muttered. 'And if any of my boys had done it, believe me, I'd know.'

'You got any ideas on who may have done it?'

'Somebody who doesn't like Minello would be my guess. I didn't like him but I don't go in for killing women.'

'Well, I hope you're on the level, Malloy, because pretty soon Minello is going to come looking for someone and when he does there'll be hell to pay.'

Malloy swallowed thickly. 'I can take care of Minello. Just where do you fit into this, Merak?' I could see he was trying to show he wasn't scared of Manzelli backing me in front of his boys. But if there'd been any more sweat on his forehead it would have been like Niagara falling in front of his face.

'That's between me and Manzelli,' I told him. I swung round and walked back to the table where Dawn was still waiting. I could feel Malloy's eyes drilling into my back. I knew that if it hadn't been for that ring there would have been a slug in my back before I'd taken a couple of steps.

'What was that all about?' she asked in a low whisper as I sat down. 'For a minute there I thought they were going to take you outside and drop you somewhere in the bay.'

I grinned. I knew a lot of the clientele in the restaurant had been watching and wondering what I could have said to Malloy to leave him in such a state.

'What — and leave you to pay the check? They claim they had no hand in Angela's murder and strangely enough I believe them. This isn't a gang killing, Dawn, although someone wants us to think it is.'

'Then who could possibly want to kill her?' Dawn broke off suddenly and turned her head quickly.

The sound of a car reached us from outside. The screech of the tires instantly told me that either somebody was late for a party — or there might be a hail of bullets coming through the window any second. I didn't stop to reason out which it might be.

Before Dawn could move I'd flung myself across the flimsy table, reached over and grabbed her arms, dragging her to the floor. The next moment the car had braked to a sudden stop. There was the sound of two shots and the window came in. Glass was flying all over us. Somewhere a woman was screaming at the top of her voice like a demented banshee.

74

Crouching down, I held my breath. Dawn uttered a muffled exclamation but kept her head down.

As the sound of the car faded along the street, I pushed myself swiftly to my feet and ran for the window. It was a stupid thing to do. My head made a perfect target for whoever was in that black car now rapidly heading for the far intersection. A moment later it had vanished.

Pulling my head back, I looked around. Several of the customers were getting to their feet, looking dazed, scarcely able to believe what had happened.

I stared across to where Malloy had been sitting. He didn't seem to be hurt but his face had gone a funny pasty colour. The two bruisers beside him were both looking up at the ceiling, their heads back, but they weren't seeing anything. Their bright red ties now matched the colour of their shirts.

Dawn walked shakily across to stand beside me. Taking out a large handkerchief, Malloy wiped his face with it. He was perspiring even more freely than before.

'Somebody's going to pay for this.' His mouth was so tight he seemed to be speaking without moving his lips. 'I don't give a damn about what Manzelli says. This time I aim to finish Rizzio for good.'

He got both hands under the table and gave a savage heave, overturning it and sending dishes crashing to the floor.

'Whoever the hitman was, he wasn't aiming to take you out, Joe,' I said soberly. 'There were only two shots and both of your men got it through the heart. I'd say if you were the target you'd have collected both slugs and your boys would still be alive. What's more, you've got no proof that Rizzio is behind this.'

'No? Then who else knows that this is my favourite restaurant or that I'd likely be here tonight? He's had me tailed here and set all of this up. Now get out of my way, Merak.'

He thrust his way past me, ignoring the two dead men at his table. Swinging savagely on me he grated, 'If you are working for Rizzio, then I repeat what I said earlier — you're a dead man. And to hell with Manzelli.'

I watched him leave. He was still scared by what had just happened — how close he'd possibly come to meeting the Grim Reaper face to face — but he was trying desperately not to show it.

Just inside the door he paused, threw a swift glance along the street in both directions and then signalled with his right hand. Moments later, a black limousine glided towards the sidewalk. It seemed to have come out of nowhere. Malloy moved quickly, pulling open the rear door, slamming it behind him. The car drifted smoothly into the night.

Glancing across at Dawn, I said, 'Somehow what's happened has put me off my food. Can we go to your place? I've got to think this out. Too many things don't tie up and I don't like dangling strings to any case, they're liable to trip you up.'

Dawn gave a quick nod of agreement and we went outside. While she signalled for a cab, I studied the street just outside the shattered window. There was something on the sidewalk.

Bending I picked it up and turned it

over in my fingers. It might have been something dropped by anyone but it was something I'd seen before — a square piece of paper with an odd symbol written on it. Once we were in the cab I showed it to Dawn.

Somehow, I guessed what she was going to say before she spoke. 'It's the same as the first one, isn't it?' I said. 'Another of those Greek letters.'

She nodded slowly. 'Yes Johnny. It's beta, the second letter of the Greek alphabet.'

'Just as I figured. Malloy wasn't the target. Whoever is behind this, they're determined to set all of the organizations in L.A. at each other's throats.'

Dawn looked worried. 'Don't you think this thing is getting too big for you, Johnny? You can't hope to stop this now, even if Manzelli is backing you.' She made to say something more but at that moment, a cab detached itself from the traffic and pulled up at the sidewalk.

We got in, gave Dawn's address and settled back. As we reached the end of the street a couple of police cars passed us, their sirens howling. I recognized Lieutenant O'Leary sitting in the first.

It hadn't taken him long to arrive on the scene and I was glad I hadn't decided to stay for the rest of the meal. At the moment I didn't feel like answering any of his questions. While Dawn switched on the electric fire and brought us a couple of drinks, I sat down in the chair beside the fire, trying to figure things out. Whoever this killer was, he seemed to know everything about his targets.

Dawn sat down in the chair next to me and crossed her legs. For a couple of minutes neither of us spoke. Then she said, 'Why were Malloy's two minders killed? It doesn't make sense. If anyone were to die, surely it would have been Malloy.'

I leaned my head back and stared at the ceiling. Those little mice were having a fine old time, running around inside my mind. The majority of gangland killings were straightforward. One of the bosses would put out a hit on someone and it would be carried out, usually without any fuss and not too much attention from the cops.

This seemed different. Neither Minello nor Malloy were the targets. In each case it was someone close to them. And after what had just happened, there was no doubt that these killings were the work of a professional. The killer had known exactly where Malloy and his men would be sitting. Even so, they were near the wall of the far side from the window and that car had stopped for only a few seconds. Yet both men had been drilled through the heart. Clearly it had been someone who was an excellent shot.

Dawn suddenly leaned forward, staring at me and I realized I hadn't answered her question. Before I could speak however, she said, 'Do you have any answers, Johnny?'

Taking a sip of my drink, I shook my head. 'I don't have any,' I replied. 'There are more dangling loose ends in this case than a hole in a sock.'

'Maybe you'll see things more clearly in the morning,' she suggested.

'Perhaps.' I finished my drink. The

warmth from the fire was making me feel drowsy. Getting up I reached for my hat.

Dawn glanced up at me and there was that lovely smile with a world of meaning in it on her lips. 'You don't have to go, Johnny.'

I knew what she meant and right at that moment it seemed the best idea in the world. 'No,' I said, 'I guess I don't.'

Putting her empty glass carefully on the table, she got to her feet, switched off the fire, and moved towards the bedroom.

4

It was early the following afternoon when I left the office and parked myself behind the wheel of the Merc. Dawn was still checking whatever leads we could find on Angela Cliveden. I didn't want either Tony Minello or Enrico Manzelli to think I'd forgotten them. If that happened there might be one less Johnny Merak in the world. Which would be a pity because I wanted to go on living for a few more years.

I'd spent most of the morning, however, running over in my mind the various places where a young boy might be concealed. I didn't like to think that time might be running out fast for him too. But knowing some of the guys Kenton was supposed to be dealing with, they might decide he was too much of embarrassment to them and hide him somewhere permanently.

Time and again, I'd tried to put myself

into Kenton's mind, trying to figure out what might be going on inside his head. From what Marcia Edwards had said, he was now in with these hoodlums so deep it would take a shovel to get him out.

I could, of course, make things a lot easier by simply going to his office and asking him outright where the kid was. But if he was the kind of guy Mrs. Edwards had painted, willing to sacrifice his own son just to get the Mobs off his back, he might not take too kindly to that approach. Finally, I'd decided that the only approach to make with Kenton was to make an appointment. Surprisingly, he'd agreed to see me.

For the first time, I realized I knew absolutely nothing about this particular case apart from what Marcia Edwards had told me. How much of it was true, I didn't know. At the moment my information was all one-sided, a little like the Tower of Pisa but with more of an angle to it. For all I knew, she might hate the guy so much for marrying her daughter, that she was willing to spin any old yarn about him.

Maybe the kid hadn't been abducted after all. Perhaps he was playing quite happily on the beach at that very moment. But I wouldn't find out by just thinking about it, sitting behind the wheel of the Merc.

Glancing at my watch if saw it was almost time for me to have a word with Kenton, just to hear his side of the story. Twisting the key in the ignition, I pulled out into the flow of traffic and headed uptown.

The Kenton building was on Main Street, an imposing edifice of white stone and a multitude of windows that gleamed brilliantly in the sunlight. The guy behind the desk informed me that it would be impossible for me to speak with Mister Kenton without an appointment. Mister Kenton was a very busy man.

I leaned forward over the highly polished desk. 'I'm also a very busy man. I do have an appointment with Mister Kenton. I think you'd better check with him. This has to do with his son.'

The guy had a pained expression on his face. It was obvious no one had spoken to him like that before and he wasn't sure what to do about it. Maybe he was wondering whether I was some kind of plain clothed cop. Swallowing hard, he asked, 'Who shall I say wishes to see Mister Kenton?'

'The name's Merak,' I told him. 'I'm a private investigator.'

Picking up the phone, he spoke into it for a couple of minutes; then put the receiver down. 'Someone will be down in a few moments to take you to Mister Kenton.'

'Thanks,' I said.

I waited. I felt like a cigarette but there was no ashtray on the desk. A few moments later, the elevator door slid open and another guy got out. He walked straight over to me.

'Mister Merak?' His tone was polite but I could tell from his expression that he didn't like the look of me and was wondering what sort of business I could possibly have with his boss.

'That's right.' I nodded and he led the way to the elevator. He thumbed a button and the door closed without a whisper. I guessed we were moving but there was no sound. The red light over the door indicated that we had reached the top floor.

Without a word my companion got out and led me along a wide corridor. Opening the door at the end, he stood on one side for me to enter. There were half a dozen girls seated at desks around the room. Several flashed me curious looks as I walked past them. All of them were good lookers and I reckoned Kenton had hand picked the lot.

At the far end was a larger desk with a tall statuesque blonde seated behind it. She, I figured, would be Kenton's private secretary. Glancing up at me, she said, 'Mister Kenton will see you in a few moments. I'll let him know you're here.'

She pressed a buzzer on her desk and a man's voice said something I didn't catch.

'Mister Merak is here to see you, Mister Kenton.'

This time I caught the words. 'Send him in, in a couple of minutes.'

Ten minutes later I was still waiting.

The secretary glanced down at her watch; then looked up. 'I think he'll be able to see you now,' she said, getting elegantly to her feet. She moved around the desk and knocked on the door before opening it.

I'd expected to see Kenton sitting at his desk but one glance over her shapely shoulder was enough to tell me the room was empty.

'That's odd.' The secretary looked all around the office. 'Where can he have gone?'

Ignoring the puzzled expression on her face I pushed past her. Nothing seemed to be out of place but some instinct told me there was something wrong. Then it hit me.

The large window behind the mahogany desk was wide open yet the temperature outside was not far above zero! The secretary made to follow me into the office, then froze as I called loudly, 'You'd better stay where you are.'

I went swiftly to the window and stared down. I hadn't realized just how far up we were and for an instant a wave of vertigo hit me. Forty storeys below a small crowd had gathered on the sidewalk and several cars had stopped. Then I just made out the figure immediately below the window, arms and legs spread out at odd angles.

A sudden scream made me jerk my head around. In spite of what I had told her, the secretary had come forward and was standing beside me, looking down.

Pushing myself away from the ledge, I said sharply, 'You'd better phone the police. Before you do, tell me where that door leads.' I pointed to the door at the side of the room.

I could see she was close to hysteria. Several of the other staff came running towards us. Finally, she managed to stutter, 'It leads to the fire escape.'

'O.K.' Grabbing her shoulders, I shook her. 'Now ring the cops — and hurry!'

I ran for the other door, pushing a number of wide-eyed women out of my way. There was a short passage beyond the door. At the end of it was a flight of stairs. Taking them two at a time, I ran down them as quickly as I could.

At the end of four flights, I came upon

a window that looked down onto a side street still far below me. There were very few pedestrians on the sidewalk but as I stood there a black limousine appeared heading from the direction of the main street. It was moving fast. Either the driver had an urgent date — or he was running away from something.

Maybe it was my suspicious mind but those little mice careering around inside my head were telling me that automobile closely resembled the car I had spotted racing from the scene when Malloy's two henchmen had been shot. I made my way slowly back up the stairs.

From somewhere outside, the distant wail of a police siren told me that someone had had the presence of mind to call the police.

Back in the office, I caught sight of Kenton's personal secretary. She was sitting slumped in a chair with one of the others bending over her.

She looked up as I approached, dabbing her eyes with a handkerchief. 'Why . . . why did he do it?' Her voice was little more than a shocked whisper.

'You reckon he killed himself?' I asked bluntly.

'What else? As far as I know there was no one else in the office with him before you came. And no one came out.'

Me — I didn't believe that for one minute. I was damned sure that Kenton hadn't taken a dive just because he was tired of life. Someone else had been in this office; someone who had helped him on his way. What O'Leary would make of it, I didn't know but a few minutes later he came strutting into the office and I knew I'd soon find out.

It didn't take him long to spot me among the crowd of near hysterical women. Pushing his way over towards me, he said in a voice like granite, 'Is this another case of yours, Merak? How is it you get always get to a place just after somebody dies?'

I shrugged. 'Let's just say I'm psychic. I know what this looks like, Lieutenant, that the poor guy jumped. But my guess is that this is a murder case.'

There was a noise a few feet away. One of the women had fainted at the word 'murder' and was now lying senseless on the floor. While a couple of others attended to her, O'Leary grabbed my arm and pulled me on to one side.

'All right, Merak, I want some answers from you and I want them now. What are you doing here? Don't give me any talk about client confidentiality or I'll haul you down to the precinct. And what in hell makes you think this is murder?'

I took out a cigarette and lit it. 'All right, Lieutenant. I'll tell you as much as I know. I'm representing Mrs. Marcia Edwards. She believes her grandson has been kidnapped by her son-in-law; the same Charles Kenton who's now lying on the sidewalk out there. I simply came here to ask Kenton a few questions and get his side of the story.'

'So why do you reckon this is murder and not suicide?'

'Because it just doesn't seem right that the guy would tell his secretary to send me in and then take a jump out of that window. He had no idea why I wanted to see him. I doubt if he even knew who I was.'

'Anything else?' O'Leary's eyes were like daggers.

'A couple of things. Anyone could have got in here through that door yonder without being seen. I've checked. It leads to the fire escape. There's a window four flights down looking out onto a side street.'

'So?'

'I spotted a black limousine speeding along that street. Whoever was driving it was in one hell of a hurry.'

'That doesn't prove anything.'

'No, it doesn't. But I think if we take a good look around here we might find something that does.'

I walked over to the large desk with O'Leary trailing after me like a dog on a leash. Nothing seemed to be in any kind of disorder; everything neatly in its place. It wasn't until I stepped back that I noticed what I was looking for; the little thing that told me everything I needed to know.

Bending, I picked up the square piece of paper that was half hidden under the desk.

Holding it by one corner, I held it out to the Lieutenant. 'Another calling card,' I said thinly. 'Left by the same person who murdered Angela Cliveden and Malloy's two boys.'

O'Leary took a small plastic bag from his pocket. I dropped the paper into it but not before I had memorized the symbol drawn on it in black ink.

'We're dealing with a serial killer here, Lieutenant,' I told him. 'It's just possible, I suppose, that Kenton was killed because of something he might have told me. Maybe about his contacts with the Mobs, I don't know. Our murderer isn't going to be easy to find. He's changing his M.O. all the time. First a knife, then a gun and now just heaving his victim out of the window.'

O'Leary looked as if the whole weight of the world had just landed on his shoulders. Finally, he muttered, 'Well, one thing's for sure. Whatever questions you were going to ask Kenton, you won't get any answers now.'

I nodded. 'Do you need me here any more, Lieutenant?' I asked.

He deliberated that for a full minute, chewing it over in his mind. Then he shook his head. 'You can go, Merak. But don't take any unexpected journeys out of town. I figure you know a lot more about these murders than you're telling me.'

Before driving back to the office, I took a trip to the waterfront. It was a maze of buildings, many of them so derelict and dilapidated it was difficult to figure out how they were still standing. The few folk I saw around were no different. This was the part of the city the rich people never saw, never knew existed.

It was also the kind of place where the Mobs might do business and a kid might be kept out of sight, locked up in some dingy office or warehouse that had been abandoned for decades.

I parked the Merc on a wide stretch of gravel and got out. There was the salty tang of the ocean in my nostrils. A couple of oldsters were seated on a small wooden jetty. Neither of them looked up as I walked over.

'Either of you fellows seen a large black limousine around here in the last couple of weeks?' I asked.

I didn't expect any answer until I'd flashed a ten-spot. Then their eyes lit up like beacons in the dark. 'Was one here about eight days ago,' muttered the shorter of the two.

'Did you see who was in it?'

'Two guys. Never seen either of 'em before,' said his companion. 'Seemed to be looking the place over. Not that there's much here to see.'

'Have you seen the car, or those men since?'

They both shook their heads.

'Did they go anywhere? Did you notice if either of them had a kid with them?'

One of the men turned slightly and pointed. 'There was no kid with them but they both went in there.'

His finger was pointing in the direction of a long, low building some four hundred yards away. It stood alone from all of the others. There were no windows I could see and only one door.

'Thanks.' I thrust the ten dollars into the taller guy's outstretched hand and then made my way towards the building.

It had clearly once been a warehouse of some kind but had long since fallen into decay. Streaks of red rust showed along the wall and there was a heavy padlock on the door.

I threw a quick glance in all directions. There was no one in sight apart from the two guys on the jetty. As I watched, they got up and started walking away. I reckoned that money might last them in alcohol until evening.

I didn't have any time to waste trying to pick that lock. Taking out the Colt, I sent a couple of shots into the metal; then pushed at the door with my shoulder. It squealed in protest but finally opened.

It was dark inside. I might have been blindfolded for all I could see. Feeling my way forward with one hand, holding the Colt tightly in the other, I moved away from the door. Only the faint sound of my shoes in the dust accompanied me.

Then, without warning, there was a flash. I caught sight of it a split second before I heard the shot and felt the scorching pain as the slug grazed my right cheek. Without thinking, I threw myself onto the hard floor, all of the air going out of my lungs as I hit the surface hard.

Jerking up my gun, I sent two shots in the direction of the flash. There was no sound to tell me that either of the slugs had found their target. Everything was as silent as the grave.

The flash had come from somewhere quite high up along the far wall and I figured there was some kind of narrow ledge there, possibly running along the entire length of the building.

Lying there, I tried to figure out who this gunman might be. Probably he simply had orders to stop anyone getting inside this place — or rather making sure they never got out again. I was lying on something that was digging painfully into my chest. Moving my free hand slowly, trying to make no noise, I felt for it.

It was a heavy crowbar. Carefully, I pulled it from under me, leaned over onto my side and threw it as hard as I could towards the far end of the building. It struck something with a loud metallic sound.

Seconds later, the hidden gunman fired

again, sending three shots into the blackness. Before the echoes had had a chance to die away, I was on my feet and running forward towards a spot immediately beneath the muzzle flashes.

It was a reckless thing to do, rushing blindly forward. In my mind, I had tried to visualize this place. Judging from the direction of the killer's shots, he was crouched somewhere on that ledge almost immediately opposite me.

I aimed at the spot where I figured he was. Praying inwardly that there wouldn't be a ricochet, I squeezed the trigger. There was a sudden gasp from above my heard and then a funny scraping sound. The next moment something thudded onto the floor almost directly in front of me.

Reaching forward, I felt around. My fingers encountered rough cloth and something warm and sticky. Whoever this guy was he wouldn't lie in ambush for anyone else.

Pushing myself onto my knees I brought out my cigarette lighter and flicked it on.

The face belonged to someone I didn't recognize. It was thin and sallow, the eyes wide open, staring straight at me but seeing nothing.

There was nothing in any of his pockets. Evidently he was someone who liked to be anonymous, possibly some hitman hired by one of the gangland bosses.

Thrusting the .38 back into my shoulder holster, I straightened up. I heard the faint sound a split second later and tried to turn. Before I could do so there was an almost inaudible swish in the air close to my head and something hit me on the side of the skull.

I dived into a sea of black nothingness.

* * *

When I finally surfaced I was sitting on something reasonably soft and there was something else against my back, holding me into a sitting position. Something made a loud noise and a moment later someone crushed into a seat beside me. There was the faint scent of perfume in the air. It was one I recognized.

With an effort, I forced my eyes open; then closed them again as brilliant sunlight sent stabs of pain through my head. A soft voice said, 'Don't try to move just yet, Johnny.' Dawn's voice!

Gritting my teeth, I opened my eyes again and turned my head with a wrench of neck muscles. For a moment, everything looked fuzzy and indistinct. Then details swam into focus.

I was sitting in the passenger seat of my old Merc. It was still parked where I'd left it, on the gravel in front of the abandoned warehouse. Dawn was leaning forward, staring at me a worried frown on her face.

'What the hell happened?' Somehow, I managed to get the words out through the incessant tattoo of the drums beating inside my skull. 'I remember putting a slug into some guy back there. Then nothing.'

'There must have been two of them.' Dawn replied. 'After you killed that first one, his companion slugged you, probably figured he'd finished you.'

I'd been lucky. My assailant had

probably been in a hurry to clear out in case someone had heard the shooting — and he'd had to carry his pal's corpse away with him to prevent a police investigation.

I put up a hand to the side of my head. There was the slick feel of blood there. 'But how the hell did I get here?'

'I carried you here and somehow managed to get you into the car.' She uttered a low laugh. 'You could do with losing a few pounds, you know.'

I stared at her in surprise. 'You carried me from that building yonder?'

'There was no one else to help and I figured I had to get you out of there as quickly as possible. There might have been more of them around.' She smiled. 'You haven't forgotten what happened with Gloria Galecchi.'

I shook my head slowly although it increased the pounding inside my skull. It had happened almost a year before when I'd been investigating Carlos Galecchi's mysterious murder in his locked vault. I'd almost forgotten the time we'd been taken on board one of the Mob's luxury yachts and Gloria had tried to rough up Dawn to get me to talk.

Gloria Galecchi had been a statuesque blonde, over six feet in her nylons, and as strong as an ox. But Dawn had knocked her out cold with a karate chop to the neck and carried her out of the room.

Beside me, Dawn got out of the car. 'Do you reckon you can drive back? I left my car over there.'

'I reckon so.' I slid sideways into the seat.

Bending, she said through the open window, 'Why the hell did you go there, Johnny? What did you expect to find in a place like that?'

'I figured it might be where Mrs. Edwards' grandson was being kept. There were two characters here when I arrived and one of them maintained that a black limousine had driven up about the time the kid was kidnapped.'

'Was there any sign of him or even any evidence he'd ever been held there?'

'None that I could see. In fact it was so dark in there I couldn't see a damned thing.'

Dawn twisted her lips slightly. 'Then all you got for your pains was a dented skull.'

'But how did you manage to find me?'

'I checked that you'd left the Kenton Building and O'Leary told me what had happened there. Fortunately he saw you leave in this direction rather than head back to the office so I figured you might be looking for places where they could have hidden that boy. That was when I spotted the Merc.'

I turned the key in the ignition. The engine started right away. I waited while Dawn walked back to her car then followed her back to the office. There were some things about both of these cases that didn't tie up.

At the office I found I had a couple of visitors waiting at the door. One I recognized at once, Marcia Edwards. The other was a much younger woman.

I let them in and pulled up another chair in front of the desk. Sitting down, I waited for Marcia to speak. From what I could see it was evident she was the dominant factor in this family. Her daughter stared down at her hands, not once meeting my eye.

'I considered it wise to come and see you again, Mister Merak,' Marcia Edwards began. 'And this time to bring my daughter with me. Naturally, in spite of what has happened to her son, Ginella is very upset by what happened to her husband.'

I leaned forward and placed the tips of my fingers together, glancing at each of the women in turn.

'I can understand it must have come as a great shock to you,' I acknowledged. 'You know, of course, that the police are treating Charles Kenton's death as murder.'

'Murder?' Ginella Edwards almost screamed the word at me. 'But we were led to believe he had committed suicide.'

I shook my head. 'It was certainly made to look that way. But we found evidence that pointed otherwise.'

'We?' Marcia raised her eyebrows slightly.

'I happened to be there when it happened. I went to have a talk with him but while I was waiting outside his office, someone was in there with him; someone who hit him over the head and then heaved him out of the window.'

'And has this someone been arrested?' Ginella asked.

'I'm afraid not. When I got into the office there was no one there. Whoever it was escaped down the fire stairs. The funny thing is, I spotted a black limousine leaving the scene in quite a hurry just after it happened.'

'So if he really was murdered it could have been anyone,' Marcia said, pressing her lips tightly together. 'Knowing the kind of man he really was, I can't honestly say I'm sorry. But as I told you earlier, he owed quite a lot of money to various mobsters who were doing him favours. That and his constant gambling.'

I could see that her daughter was on the verge of tears and motioned to Dawn who brought over a pack of tissues. Mrs. Edwards had also noticed. 'Stop your snivelling, girl,' she said sharply. 'You know how I've felt about that man for a long time. He didn't love you — he merely wanted to get his hands on your money as well as mine. And we won't be spending any money on his funeral either — his own relatives can see to that.'

Marcia looked up, her expression wretched. 'But Mother — '

'You won't be attending the funeral, either!' the older woman snapped viciously. 'I forbid it!'

After a moment she turned her attention back to me. 'I suppose Kenton's death will make things a lot more difficult for you. My grandson is still missing and if Kenton knew where he was, you won't get that information now.'

'That's true. I've reason to believe your grandson is being kept somewhere by one of the Organizations in the city. Now that Charles Kenton is dead, I'd expect whoever has him to demand a ransom from you. Have you had any telephone calls to that effect in the last day or so?'

'None whatsoever. No one has tried to get in touch with us. That's why I'm here today to find out how far you've got with this case. Do you have any leads at all?'

I rubbed my chin. It made a faint scratching noise and I realized I hadn't shaved that morning. 'That's strange,' I told her. 'Knowing the Organizations as I do, they usually demand a ransom pretty quickly, especially in case like this.'

'Unless whoever has him is afraid to make a ransom call just in case it ties them in with Charles Kenton's death,' Dawn interposed.

'That makes some kind of sense,' I agreed. 'The trouble is, so long as they hang on to the boy, the more chance there is of us finding him.' I didn't want to use the well-known phrase — dead or alive — so instead I added: 'They'll want to make as much dough out of this as possible now that his father's gone.'

Mrs. Edwards nodded slowly. 'I know I've said I won't pay a cent in ransom money but now, if they demand any, I suppose I'll have to. At least, none of it will go to that wastrel Kenton.'

I got up. 'I'm sorry I can't be of more help at the moment, Mrs. Edwards. But I assure you I'm still looking for your grandson. If I find anything, you'll be the first to know.'

She rose gracefully to her feet, stood for a moment staring down at her daughter who was still drying her eyes, then said sharply: 'I look forward to hearing from you in the very near future, Mister Merak.'

Without another word she turned and left with her daughter trailing behind her like a lost puppy.

'Not a very happy woman,' Dawn remarked dryly.

'She isn't the one who worries me,' I said.

Dawn arched her brows. 'You've got someone else on your mind?'

I gave a quick nod. 'Yeah. Minello and Malloy. It won't be long before they're at each other's throats and if one of them was in with Kenton and has the boy I wouldn't give a plugged nickel for his chances of survival.'

'You think they'll kill him?' There was a note of shock in Dawn's voice.

'You don't know these men like I do, Dawn. Even if they get their dough, they'll make sure the kid doesn't live, especially if he could recognize any of them.'

'So what can you do about it? All

Minello wants is the name of the guy who killed Angela. In case you've overlooked it, Johnny, you're still working for him.'

'Sure — but for how long? You heard what Malloy said. He's prepared to defy the Big Boss, Manzelli, and go all out against Rizzio's outfit in revenge for killing his two lieutenants.'

Dawn went back to her seat. She looked more worried than I'd ever seen her before. After a reflective pause, she said coolly, 'You know what you should concentrate on.'

'What?'

'The one thing that seems to link all of these people together — the real killer. The one who leaves his calling card behind after every murder with a Greek letter written on it. Find him and my guess is that you'll not only have a chance of getting this kid back alive — you may also stop this gang war from breaking out.'

I couldn't fault her logic. It seemed the commonsense thing to do. But what did I have on this killer? Absolutely nothing apart from the fact that he was a dead shot and drove a black limousine.

'All right,' I said finally. 'But where do we start?'

Dawn was now busily filing her nails. I knew she always did that when she was thinking. Glancing up, she said, 'Well, what exactly do we know about him? He's evidently educated and not your normal kind of hoodlum, otherwise he wouldn't be conversant with Greek. I'd say he knew quite a lot about the three people he's killed so far.'

'How do you figure that?'

She shrugged. 'From what I understand there was no sign of a forced entry or a struggle at Angela Cliveden's apartment. He knew exactly where and when Malloy would be in the Comero restaurant. And he certainly knew about that other way into Kenton's office and when he was likely to be alone.'

Rubbing my chin, I glanced down at the drawer of my desk. I felt like a drink to clear my head but I knew Dawn was watching me like a mother hen with a faintly disapproving expression on her face.

Her deductions were perfect. I couldn't argue with anything she had said. Evidently she could read my thoughts as well.

I made to say something but at that moment the phone on my desk shrilled like an angry insect. It was O'Leary and he didn't sound too happy.

'You heard the latest, Merak?'

'Are you talking about the ball game or has someone else been killed?' I asked.

'Don't try being funny with me,' he snapped. 'I'm talking about Minello.'

I sucked in a deep breath. 'Minello! What about him?' The heating was on in the office but a thin trickle of ice ran down my back.

'He's been shot. Someone tried to mow him down from a car. Since you're supposed to be working for him, I reckon you'd better get along to the County Hospital fast if you want to get anything out of him. Seems he's asking for you.'

'Then he's not dead?'

O'Leary uttered a funny sort of laugh but there was very little mirth in it. 'Not unless the dead can talk and believe me he's talking plenty.'

I put the phone down. It was the first time I'd ever heard the Lieutenant make any kind of joke. Maybe, I thought, he was human after all. Getting up, I looked over at Dawn. She had an expression of mute inquiry on her face.

'That was O'Leary,' I told her. 'Seems someone's tried to put Minello out of the picture for good. He's at the Country Hospital and wants to talk to me.'

'I'll come with you.' She got up and pulled on her heavy coat. 'This might be interesting.'

I shrugged, knowing she wouldn't take no for an answer and we went down to the Merc together.

Minello was in a separate side ward with two stony-faced cops standing outside. It was cold in the corridor and they were probably thinking they had better things to do in a warm office than guarding a hoodlum.

I went inside. O'Leary was already there standing on the far side of the bed. Minello lay there looking so white it seemed impossible he had ever had a tan.

His eyes were half closed.

'He still has a couple of slugs in him,' O'Leary remarked. 'The doc says he mustn't be excited.'

At that moment, the door opened and this guy came in wearing a white coat. I figured him for the doctor. 'I can only allow you to stay for five minutes,' he said crisply. 'We're getting the theatre ready for him now. Those bullets will have to come out if he's to have any chance of survival.'

I stepped forward until I was leaning over Minello. 'You wanted to tell me something,' I said softly.

His eyes opened a further fraction and he stared straight at me. His voice was so low I could barely make out the words. 'Malloy set this up but I'm not dead yet. I'll finish him for good this time.'

'Did you see who fired the shots?' I queried.

He gave a weak negative shake of his head. 'Too fast. It was a black limousine that came out of nowhere. But one of my boys found this in the road just after it happened.'

His left hand came out from beneath the white sheets. His fingers were tightly clasped around something. Taking his wrist in one hand, I pried his fingers open. I knew before I examined it exactly what it was — a square piece of ordinary paper with a funny symbol on it.

Straightening up, I handed it to Dawn just as O'Leary moved forward, holding out his hand. 'If that's evidence of some kind I'll take it.'

Dawn gave it to him. Smoothing it out, he stared at it. His face bore an expression I couldn't analyze. Then he said harshly, 'It's the same as those pieces of paper we found beside Angela Cliveden's body and in Kenton's office.'

'Except that symbol on it is delta, the fourth letter of the Greek alphabet,' Dawn told him. 'Somebody's taking you for a ride, Lieutenant.'

I wished I'd said that but those little mice were running madly around inside my brain. They were telling me that if this was the same killer, Malloy could have had nothing to do with this attempt on Minello's life. That same kind of calling card had been left on the sidewalk just after his two boys had been shot. I knew the same thing must have occurred to the Lieutenant but he said nothing.

When he did speak, he simply said, 'So we have three murders and one attempted killing, all committed by the same guy.'

'It certainly looks that way,' I told him.

Two guys came in at that moment wheeling a trolley. 'I'm afraid you'll all have to leave now,' said one of them.

'When will I be able to question him again?' O'Leary asked. 'There are still plenty of things I want to know.'

'I reckon you'll have to talk to the surgeon about that,' said the second guy. 'It's still going to be touch and go if he survives the surgery. Even if it's successful, it'll still be some time before he can talk to anyone.'

We all went outside into the white corridor with its sharp smell of antiseptic. The Lieutenant faced me squarely. 'So where do you come in now, Merak?' The way he said it implied that I didn't come into the picture at all. 'If Minello dies, your business with him is finished.'

'And if Minello dies, you're going to have a gang war on your hands, O'Leary. And this time, I doubt if even Manzelli can stop it.'

O'Leary's expression didn't change but I could tell he was thinking deep thoughts. Probably that possibility had never occurred to him. I reckoned it did now.

'Whatever happens, you'd better stick to finding Mrs. Edward's grandson and stay out of my hair. If Minello does live, I want you to stay away from him. Have you got that? I'll ask all the questions.' He jammed his hat more tightly onto his head and walked off without a backward glance.

'Somehow, Johnny, I think he means that,' Dawn remarked softly.

'So do I. But once Rizzio and Malloy get at each other's throats, I think he's going to regret it. I've seen it all before and I know what will happen.'

'You believe Rizzio will want a war with Malloy? After all, Angela Cliveden didn't mean anything to him.'

'Sure. But when it comes to a rival

organization trying to kill one of his henchmen, he won't stand back and do nothing. These gangs take care of their members. It's a matter of pride.'

'Pride!' The way Dawn uttered the word made it sound ugly. 'Sometimes, I wish they'd all wipe each other out and leave the rest of us in peace.'

'For once I agree with you but unfortunately if that were to happen a lot of innocent people would be caught in the crossfire. And that's what Manzelli is trying to prevent.'

I knew Dawn was thinking the same thoughts as myself. Manzelli would do everything in his power to stop any return to the anarchy of the Thirties but it would be Johnny Merak putting his head on the block.

5

Half an hour later I was back in downtown L.A. I'd put through a call to the County Hospital to ask about Minello. All I was told was that he'd had the operations to remove the lead from his body and was now as well as could be expected. Considering how close he'd come to being killed, I guessed that the Grim Reaper was still close by, waiting in the wings for him.

Things had got real messy over the past few days and I had decided that I would take O'Leary's advice and, unless any further orders came from Manzelli, concentrate on trying to find Marcia Edwards' grandson.

The fact that no call had come from the kidnappers both puzzled and worried me. If any of the Mobs had him stashed away some place, they might be getting jittery now. The longer they kept him alive in their hands, the more chance there could be that someone might stumble upon him, or he might take it into his head to make a break for it. Sometimes, unlike most adults, kids don't take the time or trouble to think things through.

I was now in a part of town that tourists and visitors to L.A. never see. The street seemed to begin nowhere and end in exactly the same place. There were rows of dingy buildings on each side. Few were occupied. The only tenants were lonely down-and-outs and rats.

Hardly any of the windows were intact, looking at the world outside through empty eyes that saw nothing. Halfway along the street was a vacant lot that was now the repository of abandoned automobiles. All had been stripped of any re-usable parts leaving only twisted, rusted shells. In the center was a couple of rusted Cadillacs, one resting on the back of the other like a couple of copulating antedeluvian monsters.

All in all, it made a depressing scene. There was an air of total abandonment about it that was made even deeper by the silence that hung over everything. It had seen better days but those times were now lost in the far distant past. Sometime, the city might decide to bulldoze the lot and put a few bars and casinos on what was left.

Yet in spite of its appearance, I knew it could make an excellent place for a small boy to be hidden.

I got out of the Merc, stretched my legs, and walked towards one of the nearer buildings. Despite the silence, I was glad of the reassuring weight of the .38 close to my left arm.

A splintered wooden door hung slant-wise on one hinge. It fell inwards as I pushed it. Dust spiralled into the unmoving air clogging my throat and nostrils. Peeling wallpaper hung on the walls like ghostly hands reaching into the room. There was nothing untoward on the ground floor and somehow I made my way up the stairs without any of them collapsing under my weight. I wasn't sure they would remain intact on my way back down.

The upper rooms were just as empty as the lower ones. Something scuttled through a hole in the corner and vanished from sight. Just one of the present-day tenants, I figured. Several of the floor-boards were missing and I eased myself carefully towards the window. There was no glass in it and I was able to put my head through and take in the whole length of the street below.

It seemed just as deserted as when I'd driven into it but then I spotted something that hadn't been there when I had arrived. About fifty yards from where I was standing, tucked away almost out of sight between two buildings, was a blue car. I could just make out the front bumper and a bit of the bonnet.

Since the Merc was parked just by the sidewalk I guessed that whoever was down there was aware I was somewhere around. It wouldn't take them long to find me — unless I found them first.

I eased the .38 in its holster, ready to jerk it out at an instant's notice. Whoever had tailed me to this place certainly wasn't here just on a house-hunting trip.

I saw the two guys a moment later. They appeared in the doorway of one of the buildings directly opposite me. I recognized the type straight away. Mean-faced men with hard eyes, their right hands very close to their jackets. They stood looking intently up and down the street for a moment; then one raised his left hand and pointed directly in my direction.

I pressed myself closer to the wall than the peeling wallpaper. These men meant business and they weren't going to leave until I was ready for the morgue. I recalled Malloy's last words to me in the Comero restaurant. He'd vowed to kill me then and now seemed the time when he was going to fulfil that threat.

Down below, the smaller guy had taken his gun from its holster. Very slowly, I did likewise. The hood seemed to be hesitating. He wasn't sure whether there was a gun on him or not and he was evidently weighing his chances of making it across the street and getting to the other side without collecting a slug.

Then his companion said something I couldn't hear and he suddenly made up his mind. Bending low, he ran forward.

He was almost halfway across the road when I aimed quickly and squeezed the trigger twice.

The first slug smashed his right wrist and sent the gun spinning away into the dust. The second took him in the knee. He uttered a shrill scream and jerked like a puppet with the string broken, dropping onto his face. I glanced back towards the shadowed doorway, knowing I'd have no further trouble from him.

The other guy was nowhere to be seen. Obviously, he wasn't the hero type. Risking his own neck to help his friend lying in the middle of the road would never enter his mind.

Seconds later there came the roar of an engine from along the street. The car appeared and headed into the distance as if all the cops in L.A. were after the driver. I eased my way down the stairs and out into the street.

The guy was trying to crawl his way through the dirt to where his gun lay near the far sidewalk. He never made it. Picking it up I thrust it into my belt.

'Damn you, Merak!' He spat the words out as though they hurt his mouth. 'I'll see you dead for this!'

Bending, I thrust the barrel of the .38 against his forehead, right between his eyes. 'I reckon you'd better start talking, punk,' I said thinly. 'I haven't got time to waste with men like you. Who sent you after me? And don't say you and your companion just came out here for a picnic.'

He licked his lips. 'You got this all wrong, Merak. Sure we work for Malloy but we — '

'Malloy threatened to kill me only a few days ago,' I said. 'And he's not the kind of guy who makes idle threats. You tailed me from my office and your orders were to make sure I never got back.' I sat down on the sidewalk, keeping the .38 trained on him.

'But there's something else you're going to tell me.'

In spite of the icy wind blowing along the street there was sweat on his face. 'Goddamnit! You damned near shot my leg off and smashed my wrist. You've got to get me to a doctor and then I'll tell you all I know.'

'I'll get you to a doctor when I'm good and ready,' I told him. 'Or maybe I'll call the cops first. I want to know whether Malloy is behind the kidnapping of Marcia Edwards' grandson and if he is where you've got the kid hidden. I'd also like to know who in Malloy's gang murdered Angela Cliveden and tried to kill Minello.'

'I don't know anything about any kid and if Malloy put out any hit on Minello and this broad he never told me.'

I shook my head. 'You're talking to the wrong guy. I know the gangs from the inside. I know how they work. Malloy gives the orders and you carry them out. Now unless you want me to smash your other wrist, you'll talk.'

I knew that if I were to get any information from this guy, it would have to be fast.

By now that other punk would be on his way back to Malloy to tell him their little plan hadn't worked out as they'd intended. Very soon, there would be a squad of cars blocking both ends of this street and I would be in the middle.

'Okay, I work for Malloy but we had nothing to do with either of these cases you're talking about. You've got to believe me, Merak. As God is my witness — '

'As far as you're concerned, God had nothing to do with it.' I made a move to slap him again with the gun butt and he cringed away. The trouble was, I reckoned he was telling the truth. Maybe I was moving along the wrong track after all.

'You know anyone who drives a big black limousine?' I asked. 'Might be a Packard or something like that.'

'No one I know personally.' The pain was now beginning to get to him and I was afraid he might lapse into unconsciousness before he answered me. Through gritted teeth, he got out, 'Manzelli has one but he never drives it himself.'

I jerked back at that. What the punk had said was true and it had never occurred to me. I'd been taken to see Manzelli twice in a car that fitted the limousine I had seen speeding away from

126

two of these crimes.

Was it likely that Manzelli himself was the shadowy figure behind all of this? It was possible, of course, that he had told me to stick with the Angela Cliveden case just to throw me off the scent. When it came to deviousness, Manzelli was the tops.

I got up. The guy was clutching his knee with his good hand and moaning softly to himself. But then a fresh sound intruded upon his mutterings — a car engine and not too far away. Without giving the hood a second look I sprinted for the Merc, slid behind the wheel, and turned the key in the ignition.

It started right away and I was moving away from the sidewalk just as the other car came into sight, sliding around the far corner. I knew better than to take the normal route back to my office. That would be the way they would be expecting me to go.

There would be cars patrolling every road and street, ready to block me off at each intersection.

Instead, I swung the Merc quickly

around the corner to my left and headed towards the coastal strip. I wasn't sure if the guys immediately on my tail would stop to check on their injured friend. It was unlikely. Once they were on the tail of someone they wanted dead, they'd simply drive right over anyone lying in the middle of the road and keep on going.

That was exactly what they did. The limousine appeared behind me a few seconds later. I could just make out the shapes of two guys in it. A moment later one of them thrust his head and shoulder through the open window.

Pulling hard on the wheel, I swung the Merc over to the other side of the road. Something hit the side of the car and went whining off into the distance. In the rear mirror, I glimpsed the killer taking aim again. This time the slug went through the rear window and embedded itself in the dashboard three inches from my right hand.

I put my foot down hard on the accelerator. There might have been some speed cops along the route but once they recognized that car chasing me, they'd usually keep their noses out of it.

Not that they considered they were shirking their public duty but if a couple of hoodlums got killed in a gang fight it just meant two less for them to worry about.

I was now on the coastal road with the speedometer needle hovering around the eighty mark. Still that car was gaining on me. Soon they would be close enough to try to sideswipe me off the road. Somewhere ahead of me was a narrow track that led up into the hills above L.A. I knew if I could reach it without getting a bullet in the back of the head I might have a chance.

These big limousines were all right on the roads but they weren't quite a good at navigating narrow twisting tracks as the one I was driving. I also doubted if either of these men knew this part of the territory.

I spotted the end of the track a couple of minutes later. It wasn't the kind of turn one should attempt when travelling at eighty but there was no other choice open to me. Gritting my teeth, I spun the wheel and uttered a little prayer. I didn't know whether God or the Devil had His mark on me at that moment but miraculously, I made it.

The tires hit loose dirt and small stones and the Merc slid sideways as I spun the wheel to counteract the skid. There was a moment when I thought the car would spin over onto its side and go rolling down the slope but, somehow, it straightened up. The tires caught and the momentum carried me up the slope.

A quick glance m the mirror told me that the move had taken my pursuers completely by surprise. I knew they wouldn't give up. By now they would be trying to reverse but I now had a lead on them and I wanted to keep it until I reached the top of the track.

Ahead of me, the trail began to climb more steeply. There were straggly bushes and low trees growing out of the dry soil on either side. The thick branches almost met overhead and at times it was like driving through a tunnel.

By the time I reached the top the guys on my tail were halfway up the slope and coming fast. On my left was a thick screen of bushes and I headed the Merc straight for them. I had only one chance and I intended to take it. Slamming my foot down on the brakes, I had the door of the car open before it slid to a halt.

Getting my legs under me I ran for the bushes and threw myself down behind them, ignoring the pain that jarred through my shoulder. Drawing the .38 from its holster, I waited as the sound of the approaching car reached me.

I guessed they were unsure of what had happened but they must have spotted my car almost at once as they topped the rise. That was when I sent three slugs into the front offside tire. The effect was immediate. I could see the driver wrestling desperately with the wheel as the car went out of control.

He almost made it. Had he cut his speed he would almost certainly have come to a halt. As it was the car now had a mind of its own. It twisted sideways. The near side rose some two feet into the air. Everything seemed to happen in slow motion as it shot over the steep side of the hill and vanished.

Getting up, I walked to the edge and looked down. The vehicle was still rolling down the hillside. It came to rest some two hundred feet below me and a moment later there was a vivid orange flash as the fuel ignited. Neither of the two guys got out.

I waited for a couple of minutes just to assure myself I'd have no more trouble from them, then holstered the gun and walked back to the Merc. The track leading down to the coastal road was empty. Some gang boss would miss two of his boys but that was as far as it would go. Nobody would come up here looking for them and none of the papers would carry any mention of an accident. Whenever anything like this had happened the organizations remained silent.

I got back to the office half an hour later to find Dawn waiting for me an anxious expression on her face. 'Where've you been, Johnny? The phone hasn't stopped ringing since you left.'

She ran her gaze over the dust all over my jacket. 'You look as though you've been through the wars.'

'I had a little trouble with some guys who figured I was pushing my nose where it wasn't wanted.' I told her.

'Malloy's men?' It sounded more like a statement than a question.

'I'm not sure. Someone gave the order to stop me — preferably permanently. A couple of hoods chased me through the hills north of here. They misjudged a sharp bend in the track and somehow finished at the bottom of the hill.'

The worried look on her face intensified. 'So two of them are dead but there'll be more after you.'

'I guess so. But at least I'm forcing them out into the open. That's all I can do at the moment. Nobody seems anxious to talk to me.'

'One of these days your luck is going to run out, Johnny.' She went back to her desk and this time there was no expression of disapproval when I took out the bottle of Scotch from the drawer and poured myself a generous measure. I suppose she thought I needed it.

After downing half of it, I asked, 'Who

was on the phone?'

'Mrs. Edwards again. She phoned three times, wanted to know if you've made any progress.'

'Anyone else?'

'Yes — some doctor from the County Hospital. Apparently Minello has recovered sufficiently for him to be discharged. He asked the doctor to give you a message.'

'And what message was that?'

'He said to tell you that Malloy is finished.'

I stared down at the whiskey in my glass. That was the last thing I wanted to hear.

'Do you know what he means?' Dawn came over and sat on the edge of my desk. Her leg brushed against mine.

'Sure. I know exactly what he means. The damned fool is still convinced that Malloy put out the hit on his girlfriend and was responsible for what happened to him. I've no doubt he'll somehow talk Rizzio into smashing Malloy and his organization.'

Dawn squeezed my arm. 'Is there no

way you can talk to Sam Rizzio and make him see sense? I know he's a gangster and a killer but when you helped get him off the hook when his boss, Galecci, was murdered, he surely owes you something for that.'

'Guys like Rizzio have short memories, Dawn. The Organization comes first every time and he'll stand by Minello one hundred per cent. You can take my word for that.'

'So there's nothing you can do?'

'I guess I can try talking to Rizzio but I doubt if it'll do any good. And I'm damned certain Malloy isn't going to be reasonable. He's always had his eye on that string of gambling joints Rizzio has downtown.'

I knew that if I were to have even the remotest chance of stopping this gang war, I'd have to act fast. The trouble was that with the big guys like Rizzio and Malloy you don't just walk into their place and ask to have a word with them. You need to phone and make an appointment — and even then you could never be sure of getting one.

I dialled Rizzio's number. It burred for several seconds and then some voice I didn't recognize came on the other end.

'Is Sam Rizzio there?' I asked as politely as possible.

'Who wants to know?'

'Johnny Merak. Private detective.'

I thought he would slam the phone down — but he didn't. Maybe there was some little spark at the back of his mind that told him that if this was important, something Rizzio wanted to know, and if he didn't put me through, he could be in big trouble.

The brief pause last long enough for him to make up his mind — sometimes this could take quite a while for these slow-witted guys who only know how to use a gun or a knife.

Evidently he had decided to play it safe for a few moments later, Rizzio came on the line. 'What is it, Merak? I understand Minello hired you to find Angela Cliveden's killer. Is this anything to do with that?'

'Only indirectly. But it's extremely important I should talk to both you and

Tony Minello. I should add I am still working on his case.'

He chewed that over for almost a minute. I could almost hear the little cogs grinding away inside his mind, trying to decide whether I had any angle for wanting this meeting and what my angle might be. Then he said, 'All right, Merak. Tony and I will be at my place at eight o'clock tonight. Just be there and this had better be good.'

'I'll be there,' I said and put down the phone.

'You're going then?' Dawn asked.

I nodded. 'Whether it will do any good, I don't know. I can but try.'

* * *

The fog was beginning to drift in from the bay as I drove along the freeway and then cut into the suburbs. In places it was so thick I seemed to be driving through cottonwool. I checked my watch. Fifteen minutes before eight. Inwardly, I wondered if I were doing the right thing taking a chance like this.

The .38 was in its usual place beneath my left arm. But I knew that would be of no help where these guys were concerned. There were strict rules. You left any artillery with one of the guys at the gate before you were allowed into the house.

It was probably a wise precaution where the big boys were concerned but it made me feel as naked as a newborn babe once my gun was taken away. There was only one thing in my favour — Manzelli's ring.

I drove past the big iron gates and parked twenty yards further on. From there I could scarcely make out the house through the fog. When you went calling on the Big Man, even if you had an appointment, you didn't just walk up to the front door and give a polite ring of the bell. You went to the gate and waited to be identified and checked in by one or a couple of their bodyguards.

In my case there were two of them. Dark, anonymous shapes that popped up from nowhere out of the fog. One of them peered closely at me as I said, 'The name's Merak. I have an appointment with Sam Rizzio and Tony Minello.'

The other guy moved to the side and said something in a low tone. I guessed he was passing my credentials along to someone higher up inside the house. If they didn't tally, I'd be sent on my way. Apparently the guy in the house was satisfied for the gorillas opened the gates for me.

Once I'd stepped inside, I was frisked and my gun taken away. I knew there was no hope of registering any protest with these guys. They had their orders and so long as I was on this side of the gates I had to go along with them.

One of the bodyguards fell into step beside me as we walked towards the front door. His companion melted into the shadows at the gate in case there were any other callers.

I suppose it was a nice touch on Rizzio's part that I was allowed in by the front door. If it had been the Big Boss Manzelli, it would have been the tradesmen's entrance round the back. But then, I'd done Rizzio one or two favours in the past and I was hoping he hadn't forgotten them.

I was taken along a wide corridor to the door at the very end. My guide knocked quietly, then opened the door and motioned me to go in. Rizzio was there, seated behind a hung mahogany desk. Tony Minello was also present seated beside him. Looking at them I felt as though I were facing the Spanish Inquisition.

'Have a seat, Merak.' Rizzio indicated the chair in front of the desk. 'We understand you want to have a talk about something important.' His tone suggested that while I might think it important, they might not and I would be simply wasting their time.

'First of all, I think you should see this,' I began, rummaging inside my pocket. 'I've already shown it to Malloy so he knows I'm on the level as far as the Organizations are concerned.'

I took out Manzelli's ring and held it out in the palm of my hand. For a moment it was as if they had both been frozen into stone — as if I were showing them Medusa's head. Then Rizzio said softly. 'Where did you get that?'

'From Manzelli, of course. Where else? You don't think I somehow got to him and took it off his finger, do you? I'd have had half a dozen slugs in my back before I'd gone a couple of yards.'

'So you're working for him?' Minello's eyes were so wide I had the impression they'd fall out at any moment.

'That's right. Don't ask me why he picked me for this job. Maybe he likes my face. Maybe I remind him of his mother or perhaps he reckons that because I'm on the outside, I stand a better chance of pulling it off.'

Rizzio leaned forward, his elbows on the desk. There was a funny look in his eyes as he asked thinly. 'And just what is this job you're carrying out for the Big Boss, Merak? I know you've had a hand in a lot of cases where the Mobs are concerned but Manzelli has never done this before, gone over our heads and brought in a private dick.'

I sat back. Somehow, I had the feeling I'd got their full attention. 'Manzelli's worried. There's someone out there who's trying to set the different Organizations at each other's throats.' I looked straight at Minello. 'First they murder your girl-friend and leave a calling card by her body. Then Malloy has both of his lieutenants killed in the Comero restaurant.

'Next Kenton, a supposedly respectable rich guy, but hand-in-hand with the Underworld, apparently takes a dive from his office window. Only we now know it wasn't suicide but murder. Then you, Tony, collect a couple of slugs fired from a fast-moving car. Naturally, you pin the blame on Malloy.'

'And what makes you so damned certain it wasn't him who planned all of this?' Minello rasped.

'Because in every case the killer left the same clue for us to find — a piece of paper with a Greek letter written on it. It's the same guy who's pulled off all of these murders. You can take it from me that Manzelli is just as sure of this as I am. It's already got to the point where Malloy wants me taken out of the equation permanently. A couple of his hoods tried to kill me today.'

Riccio leaned back in his chair and placed his fingertips together. I could see he was thinking over what I'd said. I hoped that the fact that Manzelli was behind me on this might persuade him I was on the level. If not they might soon be fishing me out of the river.

He switched his glance from me to Minello. 'What do you reckon, Tony? You figure Merak is right about this whole deal?'

Minello shrugged His face gave absolutely nothing away. It might have been carved from a block of stone for all the emotion he showed. Only his dark eyes showed anything of what he was thinking. If Malloy were responsible he would have a definite target to go after. If not, he would be chasing anonymous shadows and you couldn't gun down a shadow.

Finally, however, he made up his mind, 'All right. I'll go along with you for the time being. But if Malloy, or any of the others, try anything funny — '

Rizzio said softly, 'There's your answer, Merak,' and he smiled as he said it. 'But you have to keep your part of the bargain — keep Malloy in check and off our backs. Otherwise — ' He left the remainder of his sentence unsaid, but the meaning behind it was perfectly clear.

Unless I somehow convinced Malloy that the deaths of his two bodyguards had nothing to do with the Organizations, and Rizzio's in particular, the deal was off and, somehow, Johnny Merak was right in the middle of what happened next.

'As you've just said, Malloy has a hit out on you and I figure your chances of getting to talk with him are zero,' Rizzio said as I stood up. 'I'd like to say I wish you luck but, somehow, I don't think luck comes into it.'

I stared down at Manzelli's ring, still in my right hand. It flashed with a deep carmine in the light. 'I'm banking on this,' I said. 'Malloy was pretty sore when his lieutenants were murdered but he may have cooled down a little, especially if Manzelli's had a talk with him.'

I put the ring back in my pocket. Rizzio called something and the door behind me opened without a whisper of sound. The big guy came into the room equally silently. Rizzio nodded and I left. There was a cold sweat on my back and little fingers of ice running up and down my spine as I collected my gun and walked through the gates towards my car.

6

I felt nervous. When a guy has already made a play at killing you, you begin to wonder what might lie around the next corner. I knew there were three likely places where I might find Malloy. He had a string of nightclubs and casinos located mostly in the swanky part of town.

They were all apparently legit but that was only on the surface. More dough went out of the back of these places and into Malloy's account than anyone in authority knew about.

The main gambling joint was the Red Flamingo — and all of the clientele who frequented this joint were meticulously vetted by the guys at the front door before anyone was allowed to step onto the plush red carpet inside. If I decided to go there, only Manzelli's ring might get me inside. Whether it would get me out again in one piece was in the lap of the gods.

I knew he spent a lot of his time at home, a fancy mansion that was on a par with those of the top film stars and Hollywood producers. The third likely spot at this time of the night was, of course, the Comero.

It didn't take me long to make up my mind to try the restaurant first. There would be plenty of other folk around and if he'd enjoyed his meal it might put him in a sufficiently good mood to listen to me before he pulled a gun.

The place was packed when I arrived but I spotted an empty table near the middle of the floor. Pulling out a chair I sat down and slowly surveyed the other tables. I was in luck.

Malloy was sitting in the far corner flanked by three other guys. I guessed he'd learned his lesson and was keeping well away from the windows, his back to the wall. His eyes never stopped moving, watching everybody. I wasn't sure whether he'd seen me come in but if he had he gave no outward sign.

Then he glanced up as I approached his table. His face was hard and possibly he was having second thoughts about me. It was clear he was puzzled. My being there was something he had never expected, something he didn't quite understand. He obviously didn't expect Daniel to walk into the lion's den like this.

But then, the only thing he understood was a gun or a knife. I noticed the three guys. Two were watching him, just waiting for the order to finish me off. The third never took his eyes off me.

Then his lips twitched into what was meant to be a smile. 'I see you're a hard man to get rid of, Merak.' There was no emotion in his voice. 'I warned you the last time I'd kill you if you didn't keep your nose out of my business. It seems some people will never learn.'

I knew he was only seconds away from giving the order to take me outside and make sure I never bothered again. But something deep down inside his mind stopped him. First he wanted to know why I'd put my life on the line like this.

There was a spare chair at the nearby table and I pulled it out and sat down. I was inwardly scared to death but I tried not to show it. 'Sure you can have a couple of your boys take me outside with a gun in my back and leave it up to the cops to fish me out of the river. But I don't think you're stupid and there's something inside you wants to know why I'm here before you get rid of me.'

'All right. Why are you here?' He leaned forward a little, thinning down his lips. 'And don't think that because Manzelli is backing you in this, it'll stop me from killing you.'

'If you want to go against Manzelli, Joe, that's up to you. But I've just had a talk with Rizzio and Minello and I reckon I've convinced them that you had nothing to do with killing Angela Cliveden or trying to murder Minello. Both of your Organizations are being set up. Somebody wants to start a gang war and neither of you will come out on top.'

From the expression in his eyes, I could see that I'd finally got his attention. 'Go on.' He leaned back, tapping the top of the table with his fingers. 'See if you can convince me.'

'That evening when two of your boys were shot not more than a couple of yards from where we're sitting now, I found something outside on the sidewalk, something deliberately left by the killer.'

'And what was that?'

'A piece of paper with a Greek letter written on it.' I told him briefly about the three other calling cards the killer had left. 'Whoever this guy is, he's not one of your usual hoods. He's educated and very clever and all I know about him is that he drives a black limousine.'

'How do you know that?'

'I spotted the car speeding away just after a guy called Kenton was killed and again just after your two men were shot. Minello also identified it as the car from which he was shot.'

'Does Manzelli know anything about this?'

'You can be damned sure he does although I haven't told him — yet. But when I saw him, he was certain there's someone outside the Underworld who's setting one gang against another. He asked me to find out who this is but right now, the only clues I have are these pieces of paper and that black limousine.'

Malloy rubbed his chin. It made a thin scratching sound. His eyes never moved. They just bored right through me like a drill. He was a man who thought deep and slow — like Manzelli.

Finally, he reached a decision. 'You can guarantee that Rizzio and Minello are in on this deal? I don't trust you, Merak. Never will. But I'm willing to go along with it on one condition — you find this killer and find him quick. You got that?'

I nodded. I made to get up; then paused. 'Just one more thing, Joe. I may have asked you this before, but do you know anything about Marcia Edwards' grandson. He's still missing and it's looking extremely likely that somebody in one of the organizations has got him stashed away someplace.'

'I ain't interested in kidnapping kids even if there is dough to be made out of the likes of the Edwards family.' His eyes took on a crafty expression. 'I did hear that the kid's father had taken him.'

'Yeah,' I replied. 'I heard that too.

Unfortunately, I can't question him about it unless I get some psychic to contact him in the other world.'

The sarcasm wasn't lost on Malloy but he said nothing. It was not until I turned to leave that he said, 'I can't make you out Merak. You're in with the Feds and yet you take orders from Manzelli. Just whose side are you on?'

I grinned. 'Let's just say I'm the fall guy in the middle. I'd like to be state governor but this is the job I get paid for.'

Pursing his lips for a moment, he stared down at the snow-white tablecloth. It was impossible to tell what he was thinking. Then he gave a slight nod. 'You took a big chance coming here like this after what I said when we last met. I'll tell you what I'll do. I've got nothing against this Mrs. Edwards or the kid. I'll put out a few feelers and see if anyone knows where he might be.'

It was more than I'd expected from a guy like Malloy. 'Thanks,' I said and I genuinely meant it. 'How do I get in touch with you?'

'You don't. I know where to find you if I get anything.'

'Thanks again. I appreciate it.'

The waiter had been hovering in the background for the past couple of minutes. Malloy signalled him over and I knew it was time for me to make myself scarce. For the moment, it looked as though I could now concentrate on the case of the missing boy.

★ ★ ★

It was two days later and nothing had happened. All of my inquiries had led me only to dead ends. Two days of fruitless search and I was now beginning to believe that her grandson was no longer alive but somewhere at the bottom of the bay where only the fishes would find him.

I was sitting in the office with my feet on the desk wondering what to do next when the phone rang. Dawn had just brought my coffee over. I figured it was Marcia Edwards since some time had passed since I had heard from her — and from what I knew of her she wasn't the kind of woman to let things slide.

The voice on the other end of the line, however, wasn't her sweet tones. It was O'Leary and he didn't seem too pleased. 'Just what is it you think you're playing at, Merak?' He sounded like a dog that had lost its bone. 'I thought you were supposed to be helping Mrs. Edwards find her grandson and not poking your nose into the Mobs.'

Alarm bells started ringing inside my head as I wondered what he had found out about my meetings with Rizzio and Malloy.

I swung my legs off the desk. 'Just what are you getting at, Lieutenant?'

'You know damned well what I'm getting at. I figured from the beginning you were in deep with Rizzio and now you've been talking with Malloy.'

'And who's told you that?'

'I don't need to be told. You were seen in the Comero a couple of days ago having a nice cosy chat with him.'

I thought fast. Those little mice inside my head were telling me I could find myself in really deep trouble unless I talked myself out of this one. O'Leary wasn't the kind of man to fool around with.

'If you really want to know why I spoke to Rizzio and Malloy, Lieutenant, I was only trying to do my job. Somebody is holding the Edwards' boy and if his father was in cahoots with the Mobs, it seemed possible they might know his whereabouts. Whoever has got the kid, he's obviously somewhere where I can't find him and the Organizations are the only ones I know who can do that.'

'Then if that's the case, why hasn't there been a ransom demand?' His tone had altered slightly and I reckoned he might have accepted my explanation. 'These hoods want money and — '

'I know,' I interrupted. 'And the longer they hang on to him, the more dangerous it is for them, the more likely it is we'll find him, dead or alive.' Before he could continue, I switched the subject. 'And there's the other case — Angela Cliveden. Do you have any leads on her killer?'

There was a pause. I knew the question had thrown him a little and he was thinking on his feet just as I had done a few moments earlier. At last, he admitted, 'No we've got nothing so far. Have you found anything?'

'Just one thing, Lieutenant. I may be way off base but my guess is that whoever killed Angela and Kenton and kidnapped this kid are one and the same.'

I could picture him staring at the phone and turning that thought over in his mind. Finally, he said sourly, 'I don't know where you got that idea from but it doesn't make any sense. There's no way these two cases are connected.'

'Suit yourself, Lieutenant. But at the moment, that's how I see it.'

'You're driving up a blind alley, Merak. But I'm giving you due warning. If I hear you've been parleying with the Mobs again, I'll seriously consider having your licence revoked.'

He slammed down the phone at that. Replacing the receiver, I leaned back in my chair. Dawn said softly, 'I gather that was O'Leary and he wasn't too pleased about something.'

'He wasn't. Somehow he's got wind

that I've been talking with the big boys in the Mobs and he doesn't like it.' I lit a cigarette and blew the smoke towards the ceiling. At almost the same time, the phone shrilled again.

'Merak,' I said, hoping it wasn't O'Leary back again. It wasn't.

A voice I didn't recognize said, 'Are you the private detective working for Mrs. Marcia Edwards?'

'That's right.'

'I'm speaking on behalf of Mrs. Edwards. She would like to meet you. I understand she has some important business she wishes to discuss with you.'

His tone suggested that he could see no reason why Mrs. Edwards would want to have any business with the likes of me.

The little mice in my head woke up at that. 'And why doesn't Mrs. Edwards speak to me in person if this is so urgent? She has my phone number and knows where my office is. And just who are you?'

'My name is Pearson. I'm a lawyer and look after Mrs. Edwards' interests. She has instructed me to ask you to meet her at the corner of Main and Fifth at precisely nine o'clock this evening. Do I tell her you'll be there?'

I thought that over. I wasn't anticipating any trouble from either Rizzio or Malloy and if Manzelli wished to see me, it was an order and not a polite request.

'All right, tell her I'll be there at nine on the dot.' I put the receiver down.

Dawn gave me an interrogating look. 'Who was that?' she asked.

'He said he was some lawyer named Pearson. Mrs. Edwards wants to see me at the corner of Main and Fifth at nine this evening.'

'Did he say why she wanted to meet you there instead of here or at her place?'

'No. He just had his instructions to deliver the message.'

Her expression of anxiety increased. 'It sounds like a set-up to me, Johnny. That caller could even be the killer.'

The thought had occurred to me. Getting up I jammed my hat onto my head. 'I guess there's only one way to find out.'

'You're going?' She shook her head vehemently, her long black hair dancing on her shoulders. 'Don't be a fool, Johnny. At least let me come with you.'

I grinned. 'I reckon I can handle a sixty year old woman.'

'You've got no proof that Marcia Edwards even gave those instructions. You go there like a lamb to the slaughter and find that the butcher is waiting for you.'

'I'd like to take you with me, Dawn, just to keep me out of trouble. But I don't want to go in there having to worry about you.'

'You know very well I can look out for myself,' she said defiantly. She glanced at her watch, mentally calculating how long we had to wait, giving me no chance to stop her. I knew when she made up her mind to do something nothing would dissuade her.

It wanted fifteen minutes to nine when we left the office together and got into the car.

I let her drive while I kept my eyes open. It didn't sound like a trap to me. If anyone had arranged anything like that they wouldn't want to meet me in a public place where there were likely to be

159

pedestrians around.

Yet those little mice in my head were telling me that nine o' clock was a funny time to arrange a meeting like this in the middle of town — early enough for it not to be too dark, but late enough for not too many people to be about.

Dawn drove slowly along Main Street towards the junction with Fifth Avenue some three hundred yards away. There were a couple of cars parked near the junction. Neither of them was the black limousine I'd seen before.

'I don't see any sign of her,' I said. 'If she's the punctual type she should be somewhere in the vicinity. She was apparently insistent I should be here at precisely nine.'

Dawn indicated with her left hand. 'There's a car over there and it looks like a woman sitting behind the wheel.' Without saying anything further, she spun the wheel and parked the Merc neatly just behind the other vehicle.

I got out and went forward a step at a time because there was something here that didn't quite add up. I could just make out the silhouette of the woman in the driver's seat. She seemed to be just sitting there as if waiting for someone. It all looked quite normal and innocent yet a strange tingle brushed along my spine as I approached the car. Taking out my handkerchief so as to leave no prints on the handle, I tried the door. It was locked.

Something was wrong — but I couldn't tell what it was. Dawn got out and came to stand beside me as I leaned down and knocked loudly on the window. The woman didn't stir. For all the movement she made she might have been a statue. Swinging on Dawn, I said sharply, 'Get a flashlight. There's one in the glove compartment.'

She came running back with it a moment later. Switching it on, I shone the torchlight through the window. What I saw I didn't like. I heard Dawn's sharp intake of breath as she peered over my shoulder. The ugly bullet wound showed just beneath the woman's hair.

Her eyes were wide open, staring, but she was seeing nothing. It wasn't this, however, which sent that finger of ice

161

running up and down my spine. I recognized her. I had only seen her once — in my office. She was Marcia Edwards' daughter, Ginella!

Straightening up, I threw a quick glance along the street in both directions. There were very few folk around. Then I spotted what I was looking for. Pointing, I said, 'Get to that phone booth over there, Dawn, and ring the cops. Ask for Lieutenant O'Leary. Tell him what we've found. I reckon he'll want to be in on this personally.'

'Why him in particular?' Dawn looked surprised.

I directed the beam of the torch onto the dead woman's lap. She was clutching something small and white in her right hand. 'Unless I miss my guess, I'd say we've found another of that killer's calling cards.'

Dawn said nothing more but ran quickly across the street to the phone booth. I stood beside the car and waited.

A few moments later, a tall, thin-faced guy came out of a narrow alley, saw me and stopped. He'd obviously been drinking but he wasn't drunk.

'Something wrong, mister?' he asked, trying to see over my shoulder. Grinning, he added, 'I guess she'd had just a little too much of the hard stuff. Better get her home before the cops come.'

'They'll be here any minute now,' I replied coldly. 'And I suggest you move on unless you want to be involved in a homicide.'

His lined face changed at that. 'You reckon she's dead?'

'With a slug in her head? I'd say she's very dead.'

At that moment, Dawn came running back and there was the faint, dismal wail of police sirens in the distance coming rapidly closer. That was enough for our friend. He gave one last look and then took off quickly along the street.

'Who was that?' Dawn asked, throwing a quick glance at the man's retreating back.

'Just some nosy pedestrian,' I told her.

Two police cars drove up and parked at the sidewalk. I recognized O'Leary as he strode forward and Sergeant Kolowinski just behind him. O'Leary looked as if he had been looking forward to a quiet evening at home and wasn't too pleased at being called out.

'All right, Merak,' he grunted. 'I seem to be seeing you everywhere. You really invite trouble, don't you?'

'Not if I can help it, Lieutenant. But this is something you've got to see.' I flashed the torchlight through the car window.

O'Leary bent and peered inside. I knew his eyes were missing nothing. Finally, he pulled himself upright. 'Ginella Edwards,' he said thinly.

'Right, Lieutenant. And I guess you've seen what she's holding in her hand.'

He pressed his lips together they almost disappeared. 'If it's what I think it is, this case gets screwier every damned minute.' He motioned to Kolowinski. 'You reckon you can open this door?'

O'Leary turned to me when the Sergeant shook his head. 'Not that car, Lieutenant. It's virtually foolproof.'

Dawn took a hairpin from her hair and

handed it to me. It was the work of ten seconds to open the door.

'I won't ask where you learned that trick,' O'Leary said. He leaned inside the car and gently eased the piece of paper from between the dead woman's fingers, holding it by one corner. In the beam from the torch we all saw the symbol written on it.

'It's epsilon,' Dawn said. 'He's working his way through the Greek alphabet. Just as we figured earlier.'

O'Leary whistled thinly through his teeth as he slipped the square of paper into a plastic bag and handed it to Kolowinski. 'I want the usual pictures taken, Sergeant, and the doctor here as quickly as possible. Two of you men see that nobody comes near this car until I get back.'

'You going someplace, Lieutenant?' I asked.

He glared at me as if I'd uttered an obscenity. 'Don't you think someone should inform Mrs. Edwards of what's happened?'

I nodded. 'Sure thing, Lieutenant.

Would you mind if we tag along? I've got this funny feeling in my head. There's something here that doesn't quite add up.'

He considered that for a minute. I thought he would refuse, telling me this was police business and I should keep my nose out. But he didn't. 'Very well, but I ask all of the questions. You just keep your mouth shut.'

'I'll be as quiet as the grave,' I replied.

He obviously wasn't sure whether I was being serious or facetious but he let it pass and said nothing more. A few minutes later, Dawn and I followed him, heading towards the uptown area of L.A.

The Edwards residence stood on a high rise overlooking the bay. It was situated well away from any of the neighbours and I guessed that Mrs. Edwards preferred seclusion to the usual social life. Lights showed in several of the downstairs windows and there were more marking the edges of the drive as we drove slowly through the gates.

Dawn pulled up immediately behind O'Leary's car and we both got out. The house looked far too big for just mother and daughter but I guessed Mrs. Edwards liked a lot of servants at her beck and call. O'Leary rang the bell. There was a short pause and then the door opened. The guy who stood there was dressed in a black monkey suit with a white shirt and tie. He looked at us as though we were in the wrong place and should have gone around to the tradesmen's entrance.

His demeanour changed only a little when the Lieutenant flashed his badge. 'We're here to see Mrs. Marcia Edwards,' O'Leary said crisply. Obviously he didn't like the servant's attitude either.

'I'll see if Mrs. Edwards is in, Lieutenant.'

The butler stepped away leaving us standing outside. At least he kept the door open which was a nice touch. He came back a couple of minutes later. 'Would you come this way please.'

If he experienced any surprise at the police calling at this time of night he gave no outward sign. We followed him along a wide corridor. The plush blue carpet wouldn't have looked out of place in

Buckingham Palace. Large portraits adorned the walls and I could tell that most of them were originals.

Opening the door at the far end of the corridor, the butler stood on one side as he called out, 'Lieutenant O'Leary of the police department, Ma'am.'

Mrs. Edwards was seated in an elegant high-backed chair close to the fire. She glanced briefly at O'Leary then switched her gaze to me and for an instant, a look of surprise crossed her face.

'Mister Merak,' she said, motioning us to be seated. 'I certainly didn't expect to see you here. Have you found out anything more concerning my grandson?'

Before I could speak, O'Leary butted in. 'We're not here about your grandson, Mrs. Edwards.'

'Then who?' She looked puzzled.

O'Leary was plainly ill at ease 'I'm afraid it's your daughter.'

'Ginella? She isn't in any kind of trouble, is she?'

'I'm afraid she's dead.' O'Leary didn't look at her as he spoke but sat staring down at his knees.

'Dead? But that's impossible. I mean — how can she be? I only saw her a little over an hour ago. She said she was going into town.' Mrs. Edwards paused and then went on, 'How did it happen? A car accident? I've warned her about driving too fast and she never took the slightest notice of me.'

There was a long, uncomfortable pause before O'Leary said quietly, 'Your daughter was shot, Mrs. Edwards. We found her sitting in her car near the intersection of Main and Fifth — or rather Mister Merak found her and called us.'

'You found her?' For a second I thought I detected an accusing note in her tone. She sat very straight in her chair and it was impossible to tell anything from her face.

I nodded. 'I had a very strange phone call today. It was from a man who said he was your lawyer. The message was that you wanted to meet me at the corner of Main and Fifth at nine this evening — you had something important to discuss.'

'May I ask this person's name who phoned you?'

'Sure. He said his name was Pearson.'

She shook her head, her lips pursed into a thin line. 'I certainly know no one of that name, Mister Merak and I can assure you he is not a solicitor working for me.'

'We also found something else, Mrs. Edwards,' O'Leary said, leaning forward a little in his chair. He held out the small plastic bag containing the piece of paper. 'This was clutched tightly in her hand. It has a Greek letter written on it and it's the same as those we found at the scene of the previous four murders or an attempted murder.'

'But this doesn't make any sense.' Mrs. Edwards spread her hands in a gesture of helplessness. 'I can understand that son-in-law of mine being killed. He was working hand-in-glove with some dubious characters and I also believe he was deeply in debt to some of them. But Ginella — why her?'

'That,' O'Leary said thinly, 'is something I intend to find out. I presume your daughter had no enemies you know of?'

'None at all, Lieutenant. And if you're inferring she may have known anything of her husband's illegal business deals, I assure you she didn't. He kept her in the dark about everything.'

I shifted myself forward a little way in my chair, looking directly at her. 'But you knew, didn't you, Mrs. Edwards.'

'Of course I knew.' Her voice seemed to snap little sparks through the air. 'I knew a little before they were married and afterwards I made it my business to find out everything about him. I never wanted her to marry him in the first place.'

She abruptly switched the conversation around, away from her daughter as if Ginella was of only secondary importance to what she really had on her mind. 'Do you have any leads to follow regarding the disappearance of my grandson, Mister Merak?'

The question threw me for a moment. 'I'm afraid not. I've checked in a number of possible places if he was taken by any of the Mobs and unfortunately if it was, as you initially supposed, his father who took him, there's no way we can question him.' I paused, then went on, 'I'm afraid that it is possible you may never seen your grandson again — alive. There's always hope, of course,' I added hastily, noticing the look on her face, but — '

'But right now, I'm more interested in who killed your daughter, Mrs. Edwards,' the Lieutenant interrupted harshly. 'Finding your grandson is Merak's case at the moment. We've no proof he's dead or alive. But I came here tonight to tell you what's happened and get the answers to some questions.'

Marcia's face assumed an angry expression and she thrust her chin out at him.

'Very well. Do you have any more questions for me, Lieutenant? If not, I'd like to see my daughter.' She stood up as though defying him to refuse her request.

I could see O'Leary turning that over in his mind. It was clear he was at a loss what to do. For a moment he looked just like a schoolboy being lectured by his teacher. Clearly, he had never had to deal with anyone like Marcia Edwards before and he didn't know how to go about it.

Then he pulled himself together. 'No further questions at the moment. I think what I now have to do is put out an APB on this man Pearson who claimed to be your lawyer. If he isn't the killer, I'll bet my pension he knows quite a lot about these murders.'

7

I dropped Dawn off at her own place twenty minutes later and sat quite still behind the wheel. She glanced at me, arching her brows. 'Aren't you coming up, Johnny?'

'Not right now,' I said. 'There are a couple of things I have to check and now seems the best time.'

'Then be careful, Johnny. Until O'Leary manages to get this Pearson guy, he might decide you're getting too close to the truth and come after you.'

'I'll watch myself,' I promised. 'I'll see you in the morning.'

She looked a little disappointed but said nothing more. I watched her as she went inside and closed the door. Then I leaned back in the seat and lit a cigarette. Those little mice inside my head were really having a field day — so many questions and very few answers. I'd asked to go with the Lieutenant to Mrs.

Edwards' hoping to get some but there had been nothing.

This shadowy figure who had phoned me — my first reaction had been that if he wasn't the killer, he certainly knew who was. Now, I wasn't so sure. Either Pearson had been lying — or Mrs. Edwards was. Something kept telling me that I was looking at these killings and the kidnapping from the wrong angle. There was something here I hadn't spotted and until I did none of this would make any sense.

Tossing the cigarette butt out of the window, I switched on the ignition and drove slowly along the empty street. The police photographers would have probably finished their job by now. They would be taking Ginella Edwards to the morgue — a woman murdered for no reason I could figure out.

Somehow, I believed Marcia when she had claimed that her daughter knew nothing of her husband's connections with the Mob. So why had she been killed? I could understand the other killings — all, in some way, connected to the L.A. Organizations.

And that voice on the phone. It had belonged to someone who knew Ginella was either dead or about to be killed and also where the body would be. It wasn't a voice I would have connected with anyone in the Organizations. It was the voice of a well-educated man — the kind of man who might know Greek and yet be capable of cold-blooded murder.

I felt sure the answer to all of these questions was staring me in the face but I couldn't see it. I spotted a bar just across the street and parked in front of it. Whether the drink would clear my brain, or dull it completely, I didn't know and right at that moment, I didn't really care. I knew these two cases were beginning to get to me. I thought of a warm bed, I thought of Dawn, but the thought of a killer somewhere loose in the city overcame all of that.

Going over to the bar, I leaned on it and looked the place over, looking for a friendly face. There weren't any. The bartender sidled over. 'What'll it be, mister?'

'Bourbon on the rocks,' I said. 'And make it a large one.'

'Drowning your sorrows, friend?'

'Something like that.'

He walked off and came back with my drink a few moments later. This time there was a new look in his eyes. He leaned forward and said in a conspiratorial whisper, 'Are you Johnny Merak, the private eye?'

I felt those little mice inside my head beginning to stir. 'Who wants to know?'

The bartender jerked his head slightly. 'Fellow over there is asking about you. The little guy sitting alone in the corner.'

Without making it obvious, I studied the guy. I didn't recognize him. He might have been just a bum on the take. He certainly didn't look as if he knew who I was and wanted my help.

Picking up my glass, I walked over and sat in the chair opposite him. He sat staring straight ahead as if looking through thin air at nothing. Then he lifted his head slightly and peered straight at me.

'I'm thinking you might be Johnny

Merak, the private eye.' He spoke with a thick Irish accent.

'Then you're thinking right, friend,' I replied. 'I understand you want to talk to me. If you're wanting my help on some case, I'm afraid I'm really busy now and —'

He held up his hand. 'Nothing like that. It may just be that I'm in a position to help you.'

I ran a quick glance over him. His brown suit had certainly seen better days and it was probably the only one he had in the world. He hadn't shaved for a few days and his hair hadn't seen a comb for a long time.

I always felt suspicious of characters such as this. They sometimes had a little information but they always imagined it to be worth a lot of dough.

I leaned forward slightly so that my jacket fell open and he could see the .38 in its holster. I wanted him to know, from the very beginning, that I wasn't someone he could fool around with. His eyes widened a fraction as he caught sight of the gun but that was all. He obviously figured I wasn't going to shoot him in front of all the other customers in the bar.

Lowering his voice almost to a whisper, he said, 'I happen to know something about this case you're working on at the moment.'

'How would you know anything about that?' I asked. 'And what's more to the point, how did you know I'd be in here, unless you've been following me around town.'

His lips twitched a little in what was meant to be a smile. 'I wasn't following you particularly, Merak. I know plenty of private eyes in L.A. and quite often I'm able to help them with their cases. If you don't want my help just finish your drink at the bar.'

I leaned back, considering what he had said. I knew there were guys like him who were useful in my business for picking up bits of useful information. They made something on the side, of course. The trouble for them was that once the big boys they dished the dirt on got to hear about it, these little guys departed this world quickly and without any fuss or questions being asked.

'All right,' I said finally. 'What have you got?'

He licked his lips and his glance fell lingeringly on the empty glass on the table in front of him. I took the hint and signalled the bartender to bring a couple more drinks.

Once they arrived, he took a couple of swallows, then said softly, 'I've read about these killings in the papers and I also know that some woman was found shot in her car over in Main Street earlier tonight.'

'News certainly travels fast,' I remarked. 'How did you get to know that?'

At that question, he remained silent, looking at nothing in particular. I knew what he was waiting for. I fished inside my pocket and took out a ten-spot. He eyed it greedily like a dog that has just discovered its bone.

Taking it out of my hand, he stuffed it into his pocket, took another swallow of the whiskey; then leaned forward until his head was almost touching the table. 'I overheard these two guys talking in the

Oyster Bar a couple of nights ago. Seems they were discussing a hit that was to be carried out tonight at exactly nine o'clock. That hit was on a dame called Ginella Edwards. Does that strike a bell with you?'

I nodded. 'Sure. She is — or rather was — the daughter of Mrs. Marcia Edwards, wife of Charles Kenton. I suppose you know that he's dead too. He took a dive from his office window.'

'And she was shot in her car tonight.'

'And these two guys in the Oyster Bar — can you describe them to me?'

My informant pursed his lips and hesitated. I passed over another ten-spot and the light came back into his eyes. 'One was tall, well-dressed but not exactly the flashy type. Well-spoken guy. The other was smaller, shifty eyes, seemed like some kind of hoodlum to me.'

'That figures. You didn't get any of their names, did you?'

He shook his head.

'No, I don't suppose you would. Anyone plotting a hit like this wouldn't give anything away. And you've never seen either of these two men before?'

'I didn't say that.' His eyes had that avaricious gleam again but this time I said, 'I'm not shelling out any more dough for information. Either you tell me where you've seen them or you can talk to Lieutenant O'Leary. This is a murder inquiry and if you withhold vital information you — '

That got to him. I'd already guessed he had some kind of record and wanted nothing to do with the police. 'All right. All right. I'd sooner tell you than the cops.'

'Go on.'

'The tall snappily-dressed guy. I've seen him once or twice in the past.'

'Where?'

'Downtown. He often hangs around the big casinos there. If he isn't in with one of the Organizations, he's certainly on talking terms with them. You can't mistake him. He's a big player at the roulette and he has a scar just above his left eye. Not too noticeable but if you look close you'll see it.'

I ordered him another drink and then

left. I had a lot to think about. Things were going a little too fast for my liking.

There was a little thought at the back of my mind that wouldn't go away. Was it possible that the well-dressed guy who had placed this hit on Ginella Edwards and the so-called lawyer, Pearson, were one and the same? It made a crazy kind of sense. Certainly I now had something concrete to go on.

Those little mice, however, were telling me something different. Had it been just a coincidence I had walked into that bar and he had been waiting to spill all of this information? I didn't believe in coincidences. This had all the smell of a trap.

Either that little runt in the bar had been on the level — or the killer wanted me to get this information.

I walked over to my car, my head full of conflicting thoughts. I figured that maybe a good night's sleep might make things seem a little clearer in the morning. That was what I intended to do. But events took another course.

I had my hand on the car handle when this large limousine drew up behind the

Merc. The big guy who got out looked vaguely familiar.

'All right, Merak. You're coming with us. Get in the back and don't try any funny moves.'

I knew better than to argue. Although I couldn't be absolutely sure this was the same car I'd been taken for a ride in on a few occasions in the past, a little voice in my mind told me that these were Enrico Manzelli's boys and I had better do exactly as I was told if I valued my health.

I got in and the big guy crushed in beside me. As I'd figured we took the road out of town into the empty countryside, leaving the lights of L.A. behind us. Inwardly, I wondered why Manzelli wanted to see me. If he didn't like the way things were going, I might never see tomorrow.

I didn't ask myself how Manzelli knew exactly where to find me. As the Big Boss over all of the racketeering in the city, he knew everything almost as soon as it happened. Maybe he was regretting giving me that ring and wanted it back before he gave the order to dispose of me.

It was a chilling thought.

The drive did not take long. Although we didn't seem to be moving I reckoned the speedometer stood close to eighty of ninety all the way. There were no speed cops to make a check on us. Manzelli's car was well known and nobody interfered.

This time when I was shown into the dimly lit room, Manzelli was seated behind the large desk near the far wall. The big guy who had accompanied me stood mutely near the door.

'Sit down, Mister Merak,' Manzelli leaned forward over the desk although with his shape it wasn't easy. 'I apologise for bringing you here in such a hurry at this time of night but there are things we have to discuss.'

I said nothing, wondering what was coming next, and but waited for him to go on.

His words had an ominous ring to them.

He placed the tips of his fingers together and eyed me over the fleshy pyramid.

'First, I must congratulate you on the way you handled Rizzio and Malloy. For the moment, I believe there will be no trouble from either of them. I think you have missed your true calling. You should have been a diplomat not earning peanuts as a private detective.

'Unfortunately, however, you seem to be no closer to apprehending this mysterious killer. You can understand my position. If there are many more of these murders it will appear that I am losing control of what goes on in the city. Perhaps you can fill me in on how far you've got towards identifying him.'

I shifted uncomfortably in my chair. Inwardly, I had the feeling he knew everything down to the tiniest detail but he wanted it all and he wanted me to tell it.

Running a finger around my collar, I said, 'At the moment I do have a suspect.'

'Oh.' He feigned surprise. 'May I ask who he is?'

'He gave his name as Pearson when he phoned me, saying he was Marcia Edwards' lawyer. However, she denies all knowledge of him.'

'Pearson.' Manzelli turned the name over slowly in his mind. His thoughts moved as slowly as he did. 'That is a name I do not know. Certainly he is not a member of any of the Organizations in the city otherwise the name would be familiar to me. Is that the only reason you have for suspecting him?'

I shook my head. Strangely I was now feeling a little easier in my mind, if anyone could feel easy in Manzelli's presence. Things were going a little better than I had anticipated.

'He told me that Mrs. Edwards wished to see me at precisely nine o'clock that evening and she would be waiting near the corner of Main and Seventh Avenue.'

What might have been a smile passed across Manzelli's fleshy lips. 'And instead you found the body of Mrs. Edwards' daughter. From that you imply that he knew exactly what was going to happen, that he may indeed be the perpetrator on these killings.'

'Yes. There's also another piece of

information which I acquired just before your men picked me up.'

'And what is that?'

'Some petty crook in the bar told me he had overheard a conversation a few days ago between two men planning a hit in Ginella Edwards. I think that one of those men was Pearson.'

'Quite possible, I suppose. Yet how do you propose to apprehend this elusive man, Pearson?' His gaze drilled right into me until it seemed to scratch my back.

'I have a good description of him. Tall, educated, with a scar above his left eye.'

Manzelli mused on that for a while as thoughts moved ponderously through his mind. It was still quite possible he figured I hadn't done enough to satisfy him and my future was somewhat precarious.

'Very well, Mister Merak. I think that will be all for now. However, I look forward with keen interest to you reporting that you have finally got this killer. As you will understand, my position is extremely delicate and I do not like things which happen beyond my control.'

The meaning behind his words was

perfectly clear. Find this killer fast — or else it could be the end of Johnny Merak. I got up and felt in my pocket for the ring he had given me, wondering whether he intended I should still retain it.

He noticed the movement immediately and knew the reason behind it. 'You may keep that ring,' he said softly. 'It may come in useful to you in the future.'

After thanking him, I left with the bruiser close beside me. All in all, the meeting had been as cordial as was possible with a guy like Manzelli. The driver dropped me off where they had picked me up. Neither man in the car had said a single word during the whole of the journey. I guess they were the kind of men Manzelli liked — the strong, silent type who obeyed to the letter every order given and kept their mouths shut.

After waiting until the twin tail lights of Manzelli's car vanished around the corner I figured it was about time I got a good night's sleep. Then I'd begin the hunt for this guy Pearson who now seemed to be at the back of everything that had happened. I hadn't forgotten the main item on my agenda — finding that young kid, whether he was dead or alive.

But L.A. was a big place and somehow, I guessed that Pearson was also somehow connected with this kidnapping. What had put that idea into my mind, I didn't know. But it was there and nothing would shift it. Find Pearson, get him to talk, and I'd find this kid. It was as simple as that.

But events in my business never turn out as you would expect. I got back to my place twenty minutes later. Going up to the door, I took out my key and inserted it into the lock. The next moment there was a faint swish at my back and I dropped head first into a deep ocean of utter blackness.

Coming out of it was painful. My head throbbed as if there was a drum band beating out a tattoo in the distance. It was only with an effort that I managed to open my eyes. What little I saw told me I was nowhere near my front door. This was some place I didn't recognize. It was still dark. Holding my watch close to my eyes I forced myself to concentrate on the luminous hands. It wanted fifteen minutes to three so I'd obviously been out for quite a long time.

Whoever had sapped me and brought me here — wherever here was — seemed to be no longer in the vicinity. Either they had figured I was dead or this was somewhere too far from L.A. for me to get back in a hurry.

Getting to my knees, I hung there for a couple of minutes waiting for those little drummer boys inside my skull to quiet own. I put out my hand for something to get hold of but there was nothing there.

My ribs felt as if they had been kicked by a maddened bull and my chest hurt whenever I drew in a breath. Whoever had done this had evidently made a good job of beating me up.

Why they hadn't just shot me and left me clutching one of those calling cards, I didn't know. Maybe, I thought, this was just a warning from the killer to keep my nose out of his business and stick to helping old ladies across the road.

If that was his intention, then he sure didn't know Johnny Merak very well. I didn't give in to warnings, not from anyone. I'd taken dough from Minello and Marcia Edwards and I meant to earn it if it was the last thing I did.

Somehow, I got my legs under me and stood up fighting down a wave of dizziness. They had taken my gun — which wasn't surprising. It took all of the strength and determination I had but I started walking. There were lights, lots of them, like a constellation of tiny stars, to my left and I took it that the city lay in that direction.

The trouble was, they seemed to be a long way away and there didn't seem to be a highway in the vicinity where I might hitch a lift. I was surrounded by a bare, desolate wilderness.

There was nothing else for it. It was going to be a long walk unless I did stumble upon one of the state highways but I'd gain nothing just standing there feeling sorry for myself.

With only the faint haze of lights in the distance as my compass point I started out in that direction. An hour passed. It was the longest and most painful hour of my life. The lights seemed to come no nearer. Just keep moving, I told myself. Put one foot in front of the other and keep going.

There were times when I felt the urge to sit down and take a rest but I knew that if I did that, I would sit there until Gabriel blew his horn to herald Judgment Day.

Then, a hundred yards beyond the bottom of a stony slope, I spotted the highway. There was no traffic in sight but lights showed in the distance ten minutes later. I picked out the outline of a heavy truck heading towards town. Taking my life in my hands I stepped out onto the highway, praying that the driver's brakes and reflexes would stop him in time.

They did. He pulled up less than five feet from where I was standing.

'You trying to get yourself killed, mister, jumping onto the highway like that?'

Somehow, I made it to the cab and stood staring up at him. 'Hell,' he said. 'You look like you've been in some fight. What happened — a car smash?'

'I'll fill you in if you'll give me a ride into town,' I replied. My lips were swollen and I could only mumble the words.

Leaning sideways he opened the door and held out a hand to help me inside. I slammed the door shut behind me, wincing as a stab of pain lanced through my chest. The driver put the truck into gear before turning his head to peer at me. He was still suspicious. It wasn't every day guys like him picked up hitchhikers who looked as though they'd been moved down in a hit-and-run accident.

'The last thing I remember before finding myself in the wilderness a couple of miles back is putting the key into the door of my place in L.A.,' I told him.

He said nothing for a full minute, chewing silently on a piece of gum. Then he said, 'I guess somebody wants to see the last of you, bud.'

'You guess right. I was getting a little too close to a serial killer with a liking for classical Greek.'

He jerked his head round sharply at that. 'You a cop, mister?'

I shook my head even though it hurt my skull. 'Nope. I'm a private investigator. I reckon things like this go with the job.'

He uttered a laugh. 'You must like it. I'll say this much. It ain't as boring as my job sitting behind a wheel for eight hours a day just staring at the road.' He paused and then went on, 'Who are these guys who've taken such a dislike to you? One of the Mobs?'

'No. Just a guy with a funny sense of humour who kills people and leaves bits of paper with Greek letters on them.'

'You're kidding. He sounds like a nutcase to me.'

'Yeah,' I agreed. 'I suppose he does. Either that or he's a very clever psychopath who believes he's so smart he'll never get caught.'

After that, there was silence between us. My companion concentrated on his driving now that we were approaching the outskirts of L.A. and there was more traffic on the road.

I began to recognize streets and places and knew we were coming into the city from the north side. Finally, we stopped. 'I'm heading for the main depot now. I'll drop you off here.'

'This will do fine,' I said. 'And thanks for the lift. I appreciate it.'

'A pleasure.' He nodded. 'It always helps to have someone to talk too on these long hauls. If you want my advice, get yourself checked over by a doctor at the hospital.'

'I'll do that.' I opened the cab door and dropped onto the sidewalk. I watched as he drove off and then started walking. I knew one of the doctors at the County Hospital. He often worked night duty and I knew he could keep his mouth shut. At the moment, I didn't want anyone to know I was back in town.

The bright lights around the entrance of the County Hospital showed a quarter of an hour later.

I walked over to reception where the nurse eyed me with a faint expression of curiosity on her face as I stood in the queue waiting to be seen. Even at that hour of the morning the A. and E. Department was extremely busy with the usual drunks and those who'd taken a little too much of the white powder.

When I finally reached the desk I asked if Doctor Henson was on duty. I'd known Jim Henson for more years than I could remember and had even helped him out when his daughter went missing. I figured he owed me one.

He appeared at my shoulder a few minutes later. He looked tired but he gave a warm grin and shook my hand as he recognized me. 'What the hell happened to you, Johnny? You look as though you've been hit by a ten-ton truck.'

'I feel like it, Jim. Somebody decided to warn me off a case I'm working on and figured they'd do it the hard way.'

He took my arm and led me along a corridor. 'You'd better let me take a good look at you, Johnny.' He called to someone and ordered an X-ray.

The examination took almost two hours. By the time Henson had finished with me I felt a little better. I'd been cleaned up and a couple of stitches put into my head. Fortunately there were no ribs broken but several were badly bruised and he'd taped me up.

'I'd really like to keep you in for observations for a couple of days,' he said. 'At least those bruises on your face will disappear by the end of the week. But knowing how you operate, Johnny — '

'I feel fine now, Jim. Much as I'd like to take up your offer, I've got far too much on hand at the moment.'

'Well, just take things easy for a couple of weeks. I'll give you these tablets for the pain.' He thrust a bottle of white pills into my hand. 'Are you sure you can make it home?'

'I'll make it. And thanks for what you've done for me.'

'Anytime, Johnny. It's been too long. We should get together some time and talk over the old days.'

I left him silhouetted against the bright lights, staring after me. By the time I reached my front door the dawn was just brightening over the city. It promised to be another bright, but cold, day.

I let myself in, locked the door, and went through into the bedroom, taking a glass and a bottle of Scotch with me. Sitting on the edge of the bed I drank the whiskey slowly. It tasted good and brought a warm, soothing glow into my bruised body.

This was the first time I'd been able to think slowly and clearly without those little mice putting forward their conflicting arguments. I tried to figure out who had coshed me. Evidently I was getting much too close to that shadowy figure behind these murders.

My first thoughts were of this man Pearson. Since Mrs. Edwards had emphatically denied any knowledge of him, he had moved to the top of my list of suspects. Yet what was his connection with either the Mobs or Marcia? That was something I couldn't work out.

He must have known I'd check with Mrs. Edwards so why had he lied about himself? Had it simply been to make certain I would be the first to find Ginella's body? At that moment, it seemed to be the only logical conclusion.

That thought led me to another problem. What was his motive for killing

Ginella? When I'd first taken on this case I was certain the killer's reason for killing Angela Cliveden and Malloy's two boys was to set the Mobs at each other's throats and promote a gang war. Even Manzelli had been sure of this and he was a man who rarely made mistakes, knowing virtually everything that went on in L.A. But as far as I was aware Ginella had no connection at all with the Underworld Organizations.

I finished my drink and placed the glass on the bedside cabinet. I was just going around in circles like a dog chasing its own tail. I needed a clear head and the only way I would get my thoughts into any kind of order was to get some sleep. I undressed and slid into bed hoping for a couple of hours of complete rest.

8

Somehow, I made it to the office just after nine the next morning. Three large cups of strong black coffee and cigarettes had helped to sharpen my mental processes although physically I still felt like the wreck of the Hesperus.

Dawn took one look at me and made me sit down.

'Good God, Johnny, you look a mess. What happened to you? I thought you were going straight back to your place.'

'Oh believe me, I did. But someone was waiting for me when I got there,' I explained. 'The next thing I knew I woke up in the wilderness miles from town. Don't worry, it looks worse than it really is. Just bruised in one or two places and a lump on the back of my head the size of a melon.'

'You should see a doctor,' she said with a note of insistence in her voice.

'I have, at the County Hospital early

this morning. I managed to get a lift into town. They took my gun but fortunately I still have this.'

I opened the drawer of my desk and took out my spare revolver. 'It's more difficult to carry around but equally effective.' I placed it on the desk in front of me after checking it was loaded.

'I'll make you some more coffee.' She turned away and switched on the kettle. I knew she was thinking that if I'd spent the night with her none of this would have happened. Now, I found myself wishing I had.

She brought the coffee over a couple of minutes later and set it down in front of me, seating herself on the edge of the desk. Regarding me with a worried expression on her face, she asked, 'Do you think what happened to you has anything to do with this man, Pearson?'

'I'd think it's fairly obvious he's behind it,' I told her what I'd learned from the little runt in the bar and how Manzelli had also sent for me.

Her expression became graver with every passing second. 'You're getting into this case too deep, Johnny,' she said at last. 'Keep going like this and they'll make sure they kill you the next time.'

'I suppose that's something that goes with the job.'

She shook her head in exasperation. 'Sometimes I wonder why I bother about you. Does solving this case mean more to you than your life?'

'You know that isn't a fair question, Dawn,' I said.

She turned quickly and I could have sworn there were tears in her eyes. 'No, it isn't.' She spoke so softly I could only just make out the words. 'I'm sorry. I shouldn't have said that.'

'That's okay. If it's any comfort to you, I somehow don't think he'll try again.'

She turned quickly. She looked surprised. 'Why do you think that?'

'Because this guy is a supreme egoist. He's working to a well thought-out plan and he won't deviate from it. He's so arrogant he believes no one can stop him.'

Dawn looked dubious but said nothing because at that moment two things happened almost simultaneously.

The phone on my desk rang and the door opened and Marcia Edwards came in. I picked up the phone and waved her to the chair in front of the desk. It was Minello on the end of the line. From the sound of his voice I guessed this wasn't a purely social call.

'What's happening about that killer who shot Angela?' he demanded. 'You've had plenty of time to have some idea who it is.'

'I do have one suspect at the moment,' I told him. 'And believe me, I'm working on it.'

Whether that pleased him or not, I couldn't tell. There was no emotion in his voice as he said, 'Like I told you, Merak, just give me the name and I'll do the rest.'

I knew exactly what he meant. The guy would be picked up, quietly and without fuss, fitted with concrete shoes followed by a quick drop in the ocean.

However, I wasn't going to tell him Pearson's name, not until I had a lot more information. I needed to run this killer to earth before Minello got him, just in case I'd made a mistake. At the moment I had only suspicions and hearsay to go on and that wasn't enough for me.

'I'll give you his name once I've got more information on him,' I said.

'And when will that be?'

I thought fast aware that Mrs. Edwards was scrutinizing me closely.

'Two or three days. Then I'll have everything I need to pin these murders on him.'

'All right, Merak. That's all the time I'll give you.' He slammed the phone down. I guessed he knew I was just stalling for time.

Replacing the receiver I glanced up at my other client. 'What can I do for you, Mrs. Edwards?' I asked.

She leaned forward in the chair resting her hands on a silver cane she was carrying. 'I came to tell you that Ginella's funeral will be held tomorrow in the family plot in the churchyard. If you wish to be present, together with your assistant, you'll be welcome.'

'Thank you,' I said. 'We'll both be there.'

'Ten-thirty,' she replied. She got up. Evidently that was all she had come to tell us.

'Just one thing more before you go, Mrs. Edwards,' I said as she turned to go. 'Are you absolutely certain you know nothing of this man Pearson who claims to be your lawyer? Someone from the past, perhaps, or maybe someone hired by your late husband?'

'There is absolutely nothing wrong with my memory, Mister Merak,' she snapped. 'The name means nothing to me, nor did he ever work for my late husband.'

She went out, closing the door quietly behind her as if she didn't want anyone else in the building to know she had come to see me.

Dawn looked at me. 'Then from what she says it would appear that this Mister Pearson is our mystery man.'

Picking up the revolver, I pushed it into my belt. 'How would you like to indulge in a little gambling?'

'Gambling? I didn't know you had any time for gambling.'

'There's always a time to start,' I replied.

'I assume you're talking about these big casinos along the boulevard. Do you think they'll let us into one of those places? We don't look much like the idle rich, especially you with those bruises all over your face.'

I grinned, even though it hurt. 'If you flash enough dough around they'll let you in particularly if they figure you're a sucker for a crooked game. Beside, my guess is they'll spend all their time looking at you.'

She took that as the compliment it was meant. Smiling, she asked, 'And perhaps you'll tell me why we have to go to such places?'

'Because my informant of last night told me that our man Pearson often frequents such high-class gambling joints and from his description he shouldn't be too difficult to pick out. I want to get a good look at him if I can.'

'I see.' I didn't know whether she did or not but she fell in with my plan.

Less than an hour later, with Dawn

dressed to the nines, I parked the Merc in a narrow side street just off the boulevard. I knew it wasn't going to be easy to locate Pearson. There were more than a dozen gambling joints along the boulevard, all real classy joints run by the Organizations. Everyone knew, of course, that the roulette wheels were crooked and the dice loaded, but the rich guys from out of town, looking for some excitement, didn't seem to care.

Hundreds of thousands of dollars would exchange hands every day, most of it going one way, into the pockets of the Big Boys of the Mobs. Occasionally, the cops would raid one or two but that didn't worry the Syndicates. They paid their fines and the next day it was business as usual.

Standing outside the first one we approached were two bruisers in monkey suits trying to give the place an air of respectability. Sadly, they failed miserably.

As we came up to them, they eyed us up and down, focussing most of their attention on Dawn. One of them stepped forward but then hesitated as he noticed the wad of dollar bills just showing in the inside pocket of my jacket.

He evidently decided to ignore the bruises on my face and had us figured for rich out-of-towners looking for a good time. He nodded to his companion and we stepped inside.

The place was much larger than it appeared from the outside, filled with every kind of money-grabbing games. It was, however, the big bosses who made the dough and the punters who lost it.

Dawn and I moved among the various tables, trying to look inconspicuous but keeping our eyes open for a guy with a scar above his left eye.

There were, as always, two possibilities and I didn't want to think about either. Pearson could at that moment, be in any one of more than a dozen casinos — or he might have taken a day off gambling and be in none of them. For the first time I realized just how little I knew about this guy and his habits.

All I had to go on was what that little hoodlum had told me and I was forced to admit that for twenty bucks these guys would tell you anything. In the fifth place we tried, still without spotting anyone fitting Pearson's description, I decided on a new tactic. It was a tricky one, maybe dangerous, but at the moment we were searching for the needle in the proverbial haystack and getting nowhere.

I reckoned that if we couldn't see him, the only thing to do was ask about him. It was quite possible he was a well-known figure in these establishments. I led Dawn over to the far end of the room and said quietly, 'Since this is getting us nowhere, Dawn, I'm going to try the direct approach.'

'Meaning?'

'This place belongs to a big-time crook, Ed Callagan. I think he might talk if I ask him the right questions.'

'That could be dangerous, Johnny. Maybe Pearson doesn't like people asking about him and he could be in with this Callagan.'

'I follow. But it's worth a try and I don't want you in on this.'

'And if you don't come back?' She tried to keep the worry and anxiety out of her voice but it wasn't easy.

'I'll be back,' I promised, trying to sound more confident than I actually felt.

She watched me all the way as I walked towards the door in the side of the building. There was the usual guy standing there, apparently looking at nothing in particular, his arms folded across a chest like a barrel. I knew he was watching me closely out of the corner of his eye, his glance missing nothing.

I stopped a couple of feet from him. 'Ed Callagan in?' I asked politely.

He turned his head and looked at me as if he had never heard the name. 'Who?'

'You know who I'm talking about. Callagan owns this joint so I guess he's your boss.'

His face changed. If it were possible he looked even uglier than before. 'And just who are you, buster?' His tone intimated that if I were looking for trouble, he would be only too pleased to supply it.

'Tell him it's an old pal of his from the past, Johnny Merak.'

'Merak, you say?' He chewed my name over in his mind, trying to remember if he'd ever heard it before.

The trouble with these guys is that they don't have the brains to match their bodies and it takes a long time for even simple things to sink in. After a time, some little spark of reasoning must have told him that he'd better check with the boss before throwing me out.

'Wait here.' He turned, knocked on the door and then went in, closing it behind him.

I waited. Five minutes went by and then the door opened and he came out. 'Okay, the boss'll see you.' I guessed that Callagan had remembered me from the old days when we had both been in the Organization. The earlier note of suspicion in the bouncer's voice had changed to one of respect. Clearly, in his mind, if Callagan was willing to see someone, that person had to be someone important.

I went in. Callagan hadn't changed much since I'd last seen him several years before. He sat behind a desk near the far wall where he could keep an eye on the door, just in case of trouble. I knew there would be a gun somewhere within easy reach of his right hand.

'It's been a long time, Johnny,' he said, nodding towards a nearby chair. 'How long is it — five years, ten?'

'Something like that, Ed,' I replied, sinking into the plush chair.

'Are you still going straight?' he asked.

'As often as I can. In my line of work I sometimes have to work with both sides.'

'It must be difficult.'

I nodded. 'However, as far as the two cases I'm working on at the moment, I do have this to help me.' I fished inside my jacket pocket and took out Manzelli's ring, holding it out so he could see it clearly in the light.

Somehow, he popped his eyes back into their sockets. 'Manzelli give you that?' He seemed to have some difficulty getting the words out.

'He did. He's aware of everything I'm doing and he expects me to get whatever help I need from anyone in the Organization.'

'All right.' He leaned back in his chair. 'What is it you want from me?'

'I want some information on a guy who

calls himself Pearson. Unfortunately, that's about all I know about him except that he frequents the casinos along the boulevard most every day.'

'Pearson.' Callagan muttered the name to himself.

I nodded. 'Tall guy, well-dressed. He apparently has a moustache and a scar just above his left eye.'

Callagan shook his head. 'Can't say I know him and I know most of the guys who come here on a regular basis. The only way he'd come to my attention would be if he had a really big win or he welched on some bet he made.'

I doubted if he was lying. If I had Manzell's backing it would be extremely unwise of him give me the wrong information. He knew he had to co-operate fully or find himself in a heap of trouble.

Suddenly, he got up and went to the door and called to the guy standing outside. He spoke to him for several minutes while I waited. Closing the door behind him, he came back into the office and sat down again.

'Clem tells me he's seen some guy like

the one you're looking for. Seems he has been in here once or twice.'

'Does he know where I can find him, or where he lives?'

'No. All he knows is that he always parks his car a little way along the boulevard, never in front of the casino. It's a black Cadillac.'

'Thanks, Ed. You've been a great help. I guess I owe you one.'

Something like a smile flitted over his face as he said, 'Any time, Johnny. But if you ever feel like a flutter at the tables, go some other place. I've got my reputation to think of.'

I went back to where Dawn stood waiting for me and told her what Callagan had said. 'We're not much further on towards finding him but at least the black Cadillac could tie him in with these murders.'

9

The sun was shining brilliantly the next day and everything would have been perfect except for the strong icy wind which blew straight down from the Arctic. Dawn and I found a place a short distance from the chief mourners gathered at the graveside. They had turned up in a fleet of limousines that had followed each other in single file and with military precision.

In spite of her desire for seclusion, it seemed that Mrs. Edwards was determined to put on a grand show whenever the occasion demanded. The last time I had attended a funeral as lavish as this had been when Carlos Galecci, the racketeering boss, had been laid to rest.

Running my gaze over the assembly I wondered how many of those present had really cared about Ginella Edwards. Not many, I guessed. Most would be there merely to ingratiate themselves with Marcia.

I spotted Lieutenant O'Leary and Sergeant Kolowinski twenty yards away with the Sergeant hovering behind his boss like a shadow. I wondered if they believed — as I did — that the murderer always came to his victim's funeral.

Dawn suddenly gripped my arm tightly and inclined her head slightly to our left. There was a small knot of officials from City Hall, standing close together, and just behind them, as if not wanting to be seen, stood the guy I was looking for — Pearson! I'd never seen him before but everything fitted the description I'd been given.

He wore a black, wide-brimmed hat but even from where I stood, the scar on his forehead was clearly visible.

Taking Dawn's arm we stepped carefully among the headstones until we were standing immediately behind him. He gave no indication that he had seen us. His attention was fixed on the proceedings at the graveside.

Turning to Dawn, I whispered, 'Find

O'Leary and get him here — fast.'

She slipped quietly away without asking any questions. She was good at that — quick on the uptake.

A couple of minutes and O'Leary and Kolowinski were standing beside me. 'What the hell is it now, Merak?' he demanded. 'Your secretary says you want to see me urgently.'

Pearson had heard my name spoken. O'Leary's voice was so loud that anyone within twenty yards of us could hear it. Now he turned quickly and stared at me as if I'd just popped out of the ground.

'I've been hoping to meet you face to face for quite a time Mister Pearson,' I said. 'That is your name, isn't it?'

He had clearly recognized O'Leary. Deliberately ignoring me, he addressed the Lieutenant. 'What is all this about, Lieutenant? Have I parked my car in the wrong place?'

It was the voice I'd heard over the phone and yet —

Then it clicked. Every little piece of the jigsaw suddenly dropped into place and I knew, without a shadow of doubt, I'd got the complete picture. Watching his eyes, I said, 'This is the man you want for these murders, Lieutenant. The elusive Mister Pearson, or should I say — *Charles Kenton*!'

Both Dawn and O'Leary looked at me as if I'd suddenly lost my marbles.

'You're crazy, Merak!' O'Leary said harshly. 'You know damned well that Kenton is dead. He was pushed from the window of his office. You were there when it happened.'

'Oh, someone was pitched out of that window,' I agreed. 'But it certainly wasn't Kenton.' I turned to face him. 'I heard you over the intercom telling your secretary to ask me to wait a moment. Charles Kenton was always known for his punctuality. So why did I have to wait for ten minutes and then go in when you never answered?

'Let me tell you why as I see it. It was a very clever plan. You picked up some bum on the street and brought him to your office via the fire escape. Then you promised him a heap of dough if he would change clothes with you and pretend to be you while you would slip out on some pretext.'

'I still don't get what you're driving at, Merak,' O'Leary butted in.

'No? It was all so easy.' I spoke directly to Pearson. 'Once this poor guy was dressed as you and all of your documents were in the pockets, you sapped him, dragged him to the window and heaved him out, head first. After that, gravity did the rest all for you.

'Once he hit the sidewalk his head and face were unrecognisable. Charles Kenton was dead with that piece of paper with the Greek letter on it clutched in his fingers. Nobody would ask any awkward questions. Why should they? Everyone would swear it was you lying there. You slipped out of the office, down the fire escape, and got away in that black Cadillac I saw speeding away from the scene.'

'You can't prove any of this wild theory,' Kenton said.

'No.' My left hand moved so quickly he had only enough time to get his hands up to his chin. I think he figured I was going to knock him cold. But that wasn't what I was aiming for. Drawing my fingers along his forehead, I got a grip on the scar and pulled. It came away in my hand as did the moustache a moment later as Kolowinski grabbed him by the arms. 'I expect you paid some make-up artist to make this fake scar and moustache for you.'

'I'm quite sure there's one person here who can positively identify him as Charles Kenton,' I went on. 'The one who was going to be his next victim — Marcia Edwards.'

I guess he knew he'd drawn a bad hand. Whirling, he tried to make a break for it. But Kolowinski, who seemed to be taking little interest in the proceedings, grabbed him by the coat and pinned his arms behind him.

'Read him his rights and then take him to the precinct,' O'Leary said. 'I'll charge him with multiple first-class murder. First, I want to hear a bit more of what Merak has to say since he seems to have all the answers.'

As the Sergeant took Kenton away,

Mrs. Edwards appeared. She took one look at him and I thought she was going to faint. But she was made of sterner stuff and merely stared, open-mouthed, as he was led away.

'That was Charles Kenton, my son-in-law,' she gasped. 'But that's impossible. I thought he was dead.'

'That's what he wanted everyone to think,' I told her. 'He must have planned this for a long time. Once the Mobs started to put the pressure on him for the dough he owed them, he decided to disappear and also he made sure he had plenty of money. I think you'll find that all of your daughter's money has been transferred to some bank under the name of Pearson.

'But there was something else he wanted to do. He wanted revenge on the Organization and he decided to kill Angela Cliveden and then a couple of Malloy's men, just to arouse old hatreds and set them at each other. Ginella could have proved a danger to his plans once she discovered the money was missing, so she had to go too.'

'But why all those pieces of papers with the Greek letters written on them?' Dawn queried. 'To me it seems almost as though he wanted to be caught.'

'Quite the opposite,' I said. 'He was a supreme egoist. He left those clues to prove how much smarter he was than the cops.

'And my grandson?' Mrs. Edwards asked and there was now a little tremor in her voice. 'Did he kill him too?'

'Somehow, I don't think so. But I think we should go back to your place for the last piece of the puzzle to fall into place. I realize you'll have a lot of guests there but this is important.'

'Very well.' She nodded and walked away towards the car waiting for her.

O'Leary gave me a funny look. 'This had better be good, Merak. I'll admit you got our man but I wouldn't like to see a nice old lady like Mrs. Edwards go through much more.'

I said nothing. Knowing O'Leary all he cared about was settling this case. I didn't think he'd lose any sleep at night over Mrs. Edwards.

We reached the Edwards mansion twenty minutes later and she showed us into the large room at the front of the house overlooking the gardens. 'Please sit down,' she said. I could see that the happenings of the morning had had their effect on her but she was bearing up well.

Glancing across at me, she went on, 'Just what is it you want to tell me, Mister Merak? I came to you about my grandson. I paid you to find him. So far there's been absolutely nothing.'

'That's true,' I admitted. 'You were quite right when you said you believed the boy's father had taken him. Unfortunately, I got off on the wrong track thinking he'd been put in the hands of the Mobs. I've been looking in the wrong place for him.'

'You think you know where he is?' She leaned forward, resting her hands on the silver cane.

'Once I had Pearson figured for Kenton, everything just slotted into place. The situation he found himself in he had to make it look as if the boy had been kidnapped — for two reasons.

'First, he knew you'd hire a private investigator to look for him and thinking your grandson had been kidnapped would divert attention from his real aim — to exact revenge on the Underworld. Second, he wanted to throw suspicion on the Mobs.'

'Then where is my grandson? Kenton will never tell us.'

'My guess is he's in the last place we'd think of. You see, I don't believe your grandson ever left this house.'

She stared at me as if I'd said something utterly ridiculous. 'What do you mean — he never left this house?'

'My guess would be the cellar. Evidently Kenton kept duplicate keys to this place after you threw him out. It would be simple for him to slip in, unnoticed, at night with food for the boy and — '

Mrs. Edwards leapt from her chair with a surprising agility for a woman of her age. For a moment, I thought she was going to make a run for the door. Instead, she rang a small bell that stood on the table and a moment later one of the servants arrived. 'Get me the keys to the cellars, Dillman,' she said. 'I'd also like all of you to come with me.'

A few moments later, we followed her down the steps into the cellar. At my back, O'Leary grunted, 'You'd better be right about this, Merak.'

Thrusting the heavy key into the lock, Mrs. Edwards opened the door. Putting out a hand she switched on the light. There was a chair in the middle of the bare floor and a small figure sitting in it with a rope around his middle. His hands were tied at the back of the chair and there was a gag across his mouth.

Mrs. Edwards ran forward with Dawn beside her.

O'Leary swung round on me. There was a funny look on his face. 'All right, Merak. I guess you were right all along.' It was the nearest thing to an apology he was capable of. 'I understand how you worked out just how Kenton planned his own suicide. But how did you know he'd assumed this alias of Pearson?'

'I never forget a voice, Lieutenant. When he spoke to us in the churchyard I knew I'd heard his voice before.'

'Of course you did.' Dawn had rejoined us. 'You heard it when he phoned you claiming to be Mrs. Edwards' lawyer.'

I shook my head. 'No, I suddenly realized I'd heard it even before that phone call. That's when everything made sense. I'd heard it over the intercom on Kenton's secretary's desk. Once I realized that, I knew Pearson and Kenton were one and the same man.'

THE END

Other titles in the
Linford Mystery Library:

THE MURDERED SCHOOLGIRL

John Russell Fearn

Maria Black, Head of Roseway College for Young Ladies, and solver of crimes, is faced with a problem after her own heart when young Frances Hasleigh arrives at the college. Within days the girl is found hanged in a neighbouring wood, in circumstances that seem to be devoid of clues and without motive. When Scotland Yard is called in, Maria applies her own unique system to find a way through a maze of intrigue — and uncovers the murderer . . .

WORLD IN TORMENT

E. C. Tubb

Atomic war! It had been instituted by men — overriding the desires of women and plunging the world into destruction. Finally — the vast armies shattered, women succeed as rulers, and under successive Matriarchs the world recovers. To maintain global peace the Matriarch employs official assassins under the chief of Security Police. But when orders are issued for the assassination of the apparently harmless Don Burgarde, her personal secretary Lyra decides to intervene. The seeds of rebellion are being sown . . .

THE VENOMOUS SERPENT

Brian Ball

The brass in the Derbyshire village church depicts Sir Humphrey and Sybil de Latours. Strangely, despite the clear detail elsewhere, the face of Sybil is obliterated. However, Sally Fenton takes a rubbing to hang in the bedroom. But at night, in the moonlight, static objects begin to move — and writhe. The rubbing takes on a life of its own. Soon life in the village becomes a nightmare, and Sally and her partner are powerless to stop the evil spreading . . .

SECRET OF THE RING

John Russell Fearn

Released from Newgate jail, Dick Palmer, the son of a notorious highwayman, rides off to seek a new life outside London. However, he arrives at the village of High Beach to rest at the Black Horse Inn — and is framed for murder. Jeanette, the innkeeper's daughter, aids his escape, but like his father, he is forced to become a highwayman. Fighting to clear his name, he and Jeanette then become enmeshed in a sinister mystery involving an earlier murder . . .

DESIGNATED ASSASSIN

Frederick Nolan

Isolated in the mountains of Mourne, far from the lonely Ulster crossroads where it all began, a deadly final reckoning is in the making. Charles Garrett, lethal executive arm of the British government organisation PACT, wants revenge on the IRA assassin who mowed down his wife in a hail of bullets. Lured into a trap by a series of brutal assassinations of M15 couriers — Garrett discovers that the ultimate enemy is within. And that only he who dares . . .

A GUN TO PLAY WITH

J. F. Straker

When a series of brutal murders are committed in Sussex, Toby Vanne, an American airman on leave in Brighton, finds the dead body of a girl in a field near Lewes. She's been shot in the back with the type of revolver that was used to murder a shopkeeper in Forest Row nearby. The police call in Scotland Yard, but Toby begins his own investigation, taking into his confidence a young widow who is staying at the same hotel.